Praise for

Yukiko Motoya

and

Picnic in the Storm

"I knew immediately this book was a work of quality entertainment by a writer who had consciously worked to hone their craft—but was it literature? I had the lingering doubts of an old man now far removed from the current readership.

"Wanting to delve deeper, I decided to read it again, laying aside my long-held view of fiction: one that demarcated 'entertainment' from 'real literature.' I realized I couldn't deny it. This collection serves almost as a sampler of fresh ideas and forms, but the pieces demanded more than simply to enjoy them and then put them away, saying, 'Well, that was fun.' How is it that these pieces work with their twists and tricks, and then, on top of that, also attain the state of literature?

"The writer possesses an acuity in human observation that will be a life's work, and the prose skill to describe it concisely. After tasting the delightful surprises in each story in this varied collection, I felt not as though I had passed through a gallery hung with individual talents, but that I had seen at one glance the irrepressible formation of an artist."

—KENZABURO OE, Nobel laureate,
Oe Prize commentary on *Arashi no pikunikku*
(8 of 11 stories in *Picnic in the Storm*)

"I was impressed by how each story has a different idea, none being mere variations on a theme. It's not a book to consume in one sitting. Read carelessly and you run the risk of ending up flat on your back with no idea of what just hit you. It dawned on me that in these pieces, Motoya, already well-known for theater, was trying to achieve in fiction the gamut of what can't be done on stage. Reading this made me want to sit down and get to work. This is a collection that is provocative to writers as well."

—YASUTAKA TSUTSUI, author of *Paprika*,
Gunzo magazine on *Arashi no pikunikku*
(8 of 11 stories in *Picnic in the Storm*

"Playwright-turned-novelist Motoya has been steadily making her presence felt in the English-language market in literary magazines like *Granta*. Here she offers a deft combination of magic realism and contemporary irony . . . A whimsical story collection from a gifted writer with a keen eye and a playful sense of humor."

—*Kirkus Reviews*

"A mix of the fantastical and the painfully real."   —*The Millions*

"This inventive and chilling volume will have U.S. audiences craving more from Motoya."   —*Library Journal*

"In eleven short stories, Yukiko Motoya pulls back the curtain from everyday lives, to reveal that beneath the most mundane lies a world bizarre and alien."   —*Bustle*

PICNIC IN
THE STORM

PICNIC IN THE STORM

YUKIKO MOTOYA

Translated from the Japanese by Asa Yoneda

corsair

CORSAIR

First published in the US as *The Lonesome Bodybuilder* in 2018 by Soft Skull
First published in Great Britain in 2019 by Corsair

1 3 5 7 9 10 8 6 4 2

Arashi no Pikunikku © 2015 by Yukiko Motoya
Irui kon'in tan © 2016 by Yukiko Motoya
First published in Japan in 2015, 2016 by Kodansha Ltd., Tokyo
Publication rights for this English edition arranged through Kodansha Ltd., Tokyo
English translation copyright © 2018 by Asa Yoneda

The moral right of the author has been asserted.

The following stories have been previously published, in slightly different form:
"Fitting Room" (originally "Why I Can No Longer Look at a Picnic Blanket Without Laughing")
and "The Dogs" (*Granta*); "How to Burden the Girl" (*Tender*); and "Typhoon" (*Catapult*).

A CIP catalogue record for this book
is available from the British Library.

ISBN: 978-1-4721-5434-7

Printed and bound by CPI Group (UK) Ltd., Croydon, CR0 4YY

Papers used by Corsair are from well-managed forests
and other responsible sources.

MIX
Paper from
responsible sources
FSC® C104740
www.fsc.org

Corsair
An imprint of
Little, Brown Book Group
Carmelite House
50 Victoria Embankment
London EC4Y 0DZ

An Hachette UK Company
www.hachette.co.uk

www.littlebrown.co.uk

CONTENTS

Contents

PICNIC IN
THE STORM

The Lonesome Bodybuilder

WHEN I GOT HOME FROM THE SUPERMARKET, my husband was watching a boxing match on TV.

"I didn't know you watched this kind of thing. I never would have guessed," I said, putting down the bags of groceries on the living room table.

He made a noncommittal noise from the sofa. He seemed to be really engrossed.

"Who's winning? The big one or the little one?"

I sat on the sofa next to him and took off my scarf. I'd planned on starting dinner right away, but the gears on my bicycle hadn't been working, and I was a little tired. Just a short break. Fifteen minutes.

Eyes still glued to the TV, my husband explained that the little one was looking stronger so far. They seemed to have reached the end of a round, and the gong was clanging loudly. Both fighters were covered in blood, I guessed from getting cuts on their faces from their opponent's punches, and as soon as they sat down on the chairs in their corners, their seconds threw water over their heads.

"It's like animals bathing. So wild."

I'd tried to make sure the "wild" didn't sound too reproachful, but my husband picked up on it.

"That's the kind of man you really want, isn't it?"

"What? What are you talking about?"

"Don't pretend. I know. I know you secretly want a brute to have his way with you."

"You know I prefer intellectual men. I don't want an insensitive jock."

He put the remote he'd been clutching back on the table, then pulled up his sweater sleeve and wrapped his fingers around his wrist, as if taking his own pulse. His wrist was far thinner than the boxers', it was true.

"It's like you might be some kind of artist," I teased. He hated being pitied more than anything, so I was careful to make it sound like a joke.

"Are you saying you wouldn't go along with it, if a guy like that came on to you?"

Say something, anything, to build his confidence back up, I thought, but my attention had been stolen again by the men on the TV. My blood pumped, and I could feel my body getting hot. "Of course I wouldn't go along with it! Anyway, it's not like that would ever happen." Fighters are so beautiful. Incredible bodies, both of them. Taut bone and flesh, nothing wasted.

My husband spoke again. "What do you think of my body?"

"I like it. Your skin's so fair, and soft." Why had I never watched this kind of thing before? Boxing, pro wrestling, mixed martial arts—I'd assumed they weren't for me. How wrong I was. I always do that. I decide who I am, and never consider other possibilities. I've been like that since middle school. The time I went to the amusement park with my friends and decided that a quiet girl like me wouldn't like roller coasters, I was the only one who didn't get on the ride. Someone like me would obviously sign up for one of the cultural activities at school. Would feel at home in the crafts club. Would find a job locally. But what really would have happened if I'd gotten on the roller coaster that day? I have the feeling I would have met a version of myself I don't know now. Lived a completely different life.

The gong sounded, and the men stood up. I'd assumed that throwing out punches was all there was to it, but the boxers guarded against every blow, observing each other's movements with eagle eyes. That must be what they call dynamic vision. If only I had some dynamic vision too, I might not have missed out on so many things. The match was over, and they sounded the biggest gong yet.

The very next day, I started training to become a bodybuilder. I thought at first that I could aim to be a pro boxer, but I realized that I didn't have a trace of fighting spirit in me. No desire to beat anyone up. It was the bodies of the two boxers I'd seen on TV the previous night that seemed to be seared into my brain, even while I was at my job, working the register at a natural health and beauty shop.

They turned in all directions, showing off their bodies to me. Even while I described various products to customers. This is a moisturizing cream with pomegranate traditionally used in herbal medicine. How do firm limbs feel? This hair oil is made from rare organic concentrated plant extracts. What is it like when a strong body throbs?

Was I looking for an affair? Of course not. I loved my husband. He could be bumbling and juvenile, but he was just working too hard, that was all. I only needed to hang on until he was done with this busy period, and then he'd start initiating again. It wasn't that I wanted to touch any other man. I just wanted to luxuriate in some taut muscle. I hadn't felt so giddy in a long time. I'd swing by the pharmacy on my way home from work and get some protein powder.

•

I liked the taste of the protein powder when I tried it, and decided to join a gym. I felt a little worried about fitting it into the household budget, but I found a small, independent fitness club two train stops away, whose website advertised "100 Free Sessions Until You See the Results You Want!" Having never done any serious exercise before, I had no idea what kind of progress I'd be able to make in a hundred sessions.

On the first day of my private sessions, I confided to the trainer—a boy in his early twenties—that I wanted to become a bodybuilder. He stopped writing on his clipboard and looked at me with surprise.

"Bodybuilding? Not weight loss."

"Yes. Your website said you have a training program."

"We do, but this is pretty unusual. Women in their thirties usually come looking to lose weight, so I assumed . . ."

"Is it very difficult?"

"Not really. But with bodybuilding, you won't get anywhere with weight training alone. Nutrition is key. Could you handle consuming, say, four thousand calories a day? That's double the daily amount for an average adult male."

"I can spread it out over the day."

"What about protein powder?"

"I've already started."

"Do you have a specific goal in mind? Do you want to compete?"

"No. I don't need to show anyone. Just some muscles for myself."

"That's pretty unusual," said the polo-shirted youngster again, and then tapped the tip of his ballpoint pen on his clipboard a few times. I started to worry that he would turn me down, but then he surprised me by saying, "Okay. Let's see about coming up with a training program for you."

I found out that he'd been an athlete since childhood. He'd played rugby at university, and seriously considered becoming a dolphin trainer, but thanks to some connections he had, he ended up joining this gym as an instructor. He was a cute kid, with a boyish face. A snaggletooth. Twelve years younger than I was. He probably dressed a little dorkily when he wasn't in sportswear. That's the impression I got from his haircut. Makes sense, if he'd spent all his time playing rugby. He looked like he'd be into young women around his own age. My husband and I were the same age. We'd met in college.

The trainer, in his bright red polo shirt, looked at me soberly as these frivolous thoughts ran through my head. He said, "You need to be aware that public acceptance for bodybuilding is extremely limited. Be prepared. Also, you'll definitely need your family members to be on board."

In spite of this advice, I never did tell my husband. We'd been married seven years, and this was the first time I'd kept a big secret from him. Lately, though, he'd been spending all his time at home either buried in his work files or on his computer, and only ever talked to me when he needed me to reinflate his confidence. Marital affection was pretty much nonexistent.

I explained the change in my eating habits by saying I'd started a protein powder diet on the recommendation of one of the customers at the store. I'd tried out a lot of fad diets before, so my husband seemed not to find anything amiss. I religiously followed the training plan that I'd developed with my young coach. Hidden from my husband, who'd be holed up in the study, I did push-ups, sit-ups, squats. My basic strength began to improve, so I started to go to the gym four times a week, where I did pull-ups, dumbbell presses, narrow-grip bench presses. Reverse crunches, to add muscle definition. Ball crunches. T-bar rows. Rack pulls. Plus protein powder every few hours, and double the daily calorie intake of the average adult male.

Sculpting beautiful bundles of muscle took a lot more commitment than I'd thought. You had to reach what felt like your absolute limit, and then keep going—another two, three steps. Alone, I might have given up, but I had my coach for a hundred free sessions. Bodybuilding workouts required a partner: if you overreached on lifting a dumbbell and dropped it on your neck, you could end up dead. Coach was always by my side, making sure that didn't happen. "One last rep! You're doing great. Yes!"

By the end of a workout, I was always foaming at the mouth from breathing hard through clenched jaws. But even that felt like an exciting new discovery. When I had first gotten married, I had a hard time managing the housekeeping accounts. My husband, who brought work home even on Sundays, saw the way I let receipts pile up without dealing with them, and said, "You just have no willpower." He often berated me: "Have you ever in your life actually accomplished anything?"

The thickness of my neck was unmistakable. At the store, we demonstrate the moisturizing soaps to customers by lathering up a sample onto the backs of our hands, like whipped cream. But now all the customers were riveted by how my wrist was double the size of theirs, with well-defined tendons and veins. They pretended to pay attention to my description of jojoba oil while they looked at my neck, which was nearly as wide as my face. I could see in their eyes that they were trying to picture what they would find under my apron. It was like being stark naked.

Eventually, I got summoned by the owner of the store. "You seem a little different lately," she said. "Is something going on, dear?"

"Yes, well."

"I mean, haven't you gotten bigger, a lot bigger, than you used to be? At first I thought you might be pregnant, but . . . perhaps you're taking some kind of medication that doesn't agree with you? Something for the menopause. Are you experiencing side effects?"

"I'm not."

"But it's clear your hormones are completely out of kilter!"

I confided in the owner about my training. At first she only nodded, looking doubtful, but when I told her that I'd never felt this committed to anything before, she looked at me and said she could see it in my eyes. She was a very self-assured woman who'd raised three children on her own and managed a chain of stores. She became wholeheartedly supportive, and—knowing the old, unremarkable, unassertive me—said she much preferred the way I was now.

My coworkers at the store said that they'd help me with my fresh start too. The next day, someone brought in a yoga mat they didn't use anymore so that I could train as much as I liked behind the hair care products shelf while there were no customers around. No one batted an eyelid at me drinking raw eggs from a beer glass during breaks. Occasionally some kids would graffiti things like *WARNING smiling muscle woman will strangle you to death* on the wall of the parking lot, but almost all the customers responded positively, once they got used to it. A lot of single mothers, and women busy with careers or raising children, said they felt encouraged by my progress. I made sure I never let my smile slip, no matter how hard things got, because as a bodybuilder, I was cultivating muscle in pursuit of an ideal of beauty.

Only my husband seemed not to notice anything, even though my chest felt so solid it was as though there was a metal plate under my skin, my arms looked huge enough to snap a log in half, my waist sported a six-pack, and from a distance I looked like a big inverted triangle on legs. When I asked my coworkers for advice, they commiserated: "That's just what men are like," and "Mine doesn't even notice when I get my hair cut."

My hair was the one thing I hadn't touched, because my husband preferred it long. I tanned as dark as I could and got my teeth whitened inexpensively by a dentist a customer had introduced me to, but my hair was the same as it had been before I became a bodybuilder.

Around the time that we'd completed eighty of my four-a-week sessions, my coach encouraged me to start doing some posing. "I know it feels good to be getting bigger, but you should compete and get some people to see you. It'll be something to aim for," he said.

The first few times he suggested it, I politely refused, saying big occasions like that weren't my style, but my coach kept at it. "I really think we need to do something about your deep-seated lack of self-belief."

"Lack of self-belief? Mine?"

"Yes. Maybe you don't see it, but you're always mumbling 'anyway' after everything you say, or talking about 'the kind of person you are.' I don't know where that comes from, but I think you need to get your confidence back."

I knew the reason. Living with my perfectionist husband had made me think that I was a person with no redeeming qualities. It hadn't been like that before we were married, but gradually, as I constantly tried to compensate for his lack of confidence by listing all my own faults, I'd acquired the habit of dismissing myself.

"I can't promise that I'll compete," I said, striking a pose for the first time in my life in front of the gym's mirror. This was what being a bodybuilder was all about. Nervously I brought my arms up beside my face and held myself at the angle that made them look the most impressive.

"Make it look easy!" said my coach, so I lifted up the corners of my mouth and kept trying my best to flaunt my muscles.

My smile was still a little unsure. I dropped the pose without having been able to look my mirror self in the eye.

"There's no rush. We'll work on it together," my coach said, and draped a towel over my shoulders.

One day, while I was giving out samples of jojoba oil near the store entrance, a fight broke out just outside between two of our customers' dogs. The Yorkie's collar broke off from its leash, and the little dog approached the much bigger dog, yapping loudly, which made the big dog pick him up by the neck. The big dog was a timid dog, the kind that would normally look around at a loss rather than get angry when another dog approached it sniffing and growling. The Yorkie's owner tried to rescue her pet and, in desperation, hit the big dog with the Yorkie's leash, which made the big dog even more confused and agitated, and it shook its head from side to side, still holding the little dog in its jaws. The Yorkie's yapping got quieter and quieter, and by the time the big dog opened its jaws and unhooked its fangs, the unfortunate puppy had already breathed its last breath.

No one said a thing, but I knew what they were thinking: Why hadn't I—who'd been the nearest to the scene—pulled the two dogs apart, using my log-like arms? Why should they continue to lend support to muscles that were useless when they were really needed?

A bodybuilder's muscles are different from an athlete's. They exist purely for aesthetic value. A proud bodybuilder never puts their power to practical use. Because I'd bought into these beliefs, it hadn't even crossed my mind to stop the dogs from fighting. None of this needed to have happened if I'd stepped in and broken them up. The Yorkie had been a friendly, energetic puppy, popular at the store, and I'd held him in my arms a few times too.

"I'll stop training at the store from now on." I told the owner this before I headed home for the day, and she nodded, saying maybe that was for the best. In the staff room, no one spoke to me. The atmosphere was strained. I said, "See you tomorrow," and everyone replied, "Take care," but as I passed the back of the store, I saw the yoga mat thrown out in the trash.

After dinner, just as my husband was about to go back to the study, I said to him, "There was an incident at work today." Witnessing the death of that Yorkie had shaken me more than I'd realized. I told him my worries, wondering whether I'd be able to keep working at the store, but he responded as usual with "Hmm" and "Right," and then stood up to go.

I noticed myself feeling incredibly angry. Picking the bread-crumbs off the table and gathering the dishes, I said, "I went to the salon today." Before I knew it, I was holding up a strand of hair and saying, "I got it cut pretty short." I hadn't been to the salon in months.

My husband paused in the middle of pushing his chair back to the table, and looked me over. I couldn't remember the last time he'd looked at me like that. He had a few more wrinkles on his face, but other than that, he'd hardly changed since college. Just the same as when we met at nineteen. After a moment, he said, "Looks good."

"Really? I thought you liked my hair long."

"This isn't bad either."

"How much do you think I got cut?"

"Hmm. Around eight inches?" He scratched the side of his nose. Then, perhaps noticing my strained expression, he smiled, as though to placate me. This was the smile I'd once found so appealing that I'd given in to his earnest invitations to go out with him, despite having been interested in someone else at the time. Surprised at the tears that fell one after the other down my cheeks, my husband said, "What's wrong?"

I went to wipe my eyes, but because of the tanning oil I'd slathered on earlier, the tears traveled smoothly down my arm.

"It's nothing."

"But you're crying. Did you have a bad day at work?"

He'd completely forgotten that I'd been telling him all about it until just a minute ago. When I shook my head, he moved around the table to my side and awkwardly stroked my shoulder. But my deltoid muscles were beautifully filled in from doing rack pulls, and it felt less like him comforting me and more like me letting him admire my physique. No. I couldn't do this anymore.

I took his little hand and said, "You only care about yourself. The longer I'm with you, the more unsure I become of myself. Am I really that uninteresting?"

My husband didn't seem to understand why I was so upset. I pursed my lips to stop the flow of tears, and took off my knit top and skirt, right in front of his eyes. Seeing the micro bikini I'd worn for practicing my posing, my husband said tentatively, "What's that? Lingerie?"

I left the house. There was still time before the gym closed. Coach. Coach, Coach!

Even though I arrived breathless and in my bikini, Coach let me into the gym with a smile.

"I want to train."

"But overtraining has real risks. You've got to rest up on your rest days."

"Just three sets of bench presses. They make me feel relaxed."

I kept pleading with him, so Coach said, "Very well," and let me get on the bench.

As I lifted and lowered the barbell in the deserted gym, the tears spilled from my eyes. "He just doesn't understand."

"Your partner?"

"Yes. He doesn't understand anything."

"Have you tried talking to him?"

"I can't. My husband's not interested in me."

"You still have to talk. Bodybuilding's lonely at the best of times."

Lonely. Coach's word caught in my chest.

"I don't know how to get through to him."

I let go of the barbell, covered my face with my hands, and let slip something that should never have been said. "I wish you were my partner, Coach."

Coach took my comment in silence. I knew he valued me as a client, so I didn't say anything more. But how many times had I thought, while training, that he was much more of a partner to me than my husband? He helped me achieve things beyond my own limits, and was even more passionate than I was about my progress.

After a while, Coach said, "Better now?"

Thanks to him tactfully implying I hadn't really meant what I said, I was able to nod and take hold of the barbell again.

"Of all athletes, I most respect bodybuilders, because there's no one more solitary. They hide their deep loneliness, and give everyone a smile. Showing their teeth, all the time, as if they have no other feelings. It's an expression of how hard life is, and their determination to keep going anyway."

"But," I said, to Coach's quiet words, "if you're always smiling like that, don't you lose sight of your true feelings? Is it right to smile when really you're so lonely you could cry? I . . . I wish now I could have shown my husband all my different faces. There's so much inside me he doesn't know."

I guess I won't come here to train anymore, I thought. I'll divorce my husband, go back to being an average, boring woman, and spend an eternity slowly dying while I wonder whether things would have been different if I'd gotten on that roller coaster when I was in middle school.

Thump thump thump. At the dull noise, Coach went toward the big glass window. I sat up on the bench too. My husband was on the other side of the glass, striking it desperately with his fists.

"Is that your husband?" Coach asked, and I said, "Yes," in a slight daze.

How had he gotten here? He didn't know about my gym. I'd never seen him so visibly upset before.

Coach said, "I'll let him in by the back entrance," and left the training room, and once he was gone I didn't know what to do. My husband had caught me alone with my young personal trainer. He was so worked up. Was he going to shout at me? But part of me was ready for it. When I understood that this was the moment everything would finally become clear, the waiting seemed to take forever. My husband was still hitting the glass.

I stood up and went to the window, and nervously struck a pose at him. Both arms up and bent by my head, chest out, emphasizing my V-taper. My husband looked incredulous as I posed in my bikini. When I put my fists by my hips, striking another pose, he shook his head, looking pained, as if to say, *Please, no more.* I knew he'd never wanted to see his wife like this. But this was the real me. Still holding my pose, I showed him all the expressions I'd never shown him before. My lonely face, my sad face, my indifferent face. My face when I thought his technique was lacking. *This is me,* I tried to tell him. I'm not a boring housewife. I'm not the kind of wife her husband would ignore.

Coach must have called to him, because my husband went off toward the back door. My strength evaporated, and I sat down. I couldn't think about anything until Coach knocked on the training room door.

"I've brought your husband. The two of you need to talk. You're so much alike . . ."

As I wondered what Coach meant by that, my husband appeared from behind him. Instinctively, I was on my guard, but he wasn't angry. He wasn't crying either. He looked at me with a worried, uncertain expression and walked toward me until he was by my side.

"I didn't notice, until I found your gym membership card . . . that you'd gotten so big."

He held me tight and stroked my hair, over and over.

I still work out, and on sunny days I sometimes put on some tanning lotion and head to the park with my husband. We gaze at the dog park and eat chicken sandwiches, and even sometimes hold hands as we walk over fallen leaves. His hands are still as slender as an artist's, and my arms are chunky like a wild beast's, thanks to my training. Passersby always do a double take at the contrast between our physiques, but we don't give it a second thought.

Coach says my posing has really improved. "I get the sense you've had some kind of breakthrough."

The store owner has smoothed over my relationship with my coworkers too. They say I should enter a bodybuilding competition, but I don't know yet whether I will or not. They say that if I do, they'll form a fan club and get me a fancy banner. At lunch break today, someone said, "I guess we should take your wishes into account. What would you like for it to say?"

I said, "How about: *You can now fling any roller coaster with your bare hands!*"

I want to increase my barbell lifts by another thirty pounds before spring. And I want to get a dog, an adorable Yorkie.

Fitting Room

SHE'D GONE IN, SO THERE WAS NO WAY SHE wasn't coming out again. The only things in there were a rug and a mirror. But the customer had already been in the fitting room for three hours.

What was she doing in there? Trying on our clothes, of course. Nonstop, since midafternoon. Whenever I asked her, "How are you doing in there, madam?" she'd reply, "I'm just getting changed." When a customer says this, you really have to wait a while before asking again—because if you do and they have to say "I'm just getting changed" again, that would feel really awkward, as if you'd been trying to rush them; plus, they'd probably be insinuating that they were doing things at their own pace and wanted you to leave them alone.

In terms of reasons a customer might not come out of the fitting room, one possibility is that they've actually finished changing but the clothes are hopelessly unsuitable. It's happened to me too: there are some clothes in the world that, the moment you put them on, make you feel so miserable you just want to smash the mirror in front of you as your reflection looks on in surprise. The kind of clothes that make you think, *You've got to be kidding*, and wonder if perhaps you've always looked like a clown, whether your entire life up until that point has been an embarrassing mistake.

At first, I thought that must be it. The shop where I work mainly sells slightly quirky pieces from high-fashion labels that the owner purchases overseas, so it's not uncommon for a customer to try something on but then feel hesitant about coming out of the booth to look at herself in the large mirror. Our clothes are by no means inexpensive either, so when that happens, we tend to leave the customer be and give her plenty of time to make up her mind in private. So I was ringing up other customers, and organizing the stock room, and generally trying to fill some time before checking up on the customer again.

When I couldn't wait any longer, I called through the curtain, "Is there anything I can help you with at all?"

"There's nothing. I'm fine," said the customer, sounding a little annoyed. "But haven't you got a dress that's more casual than this one? This one is too much of a party dress. I couldn't just wear it anywhere."

"In that case," I said, and brought her a light silk dress with a subtle, almost translucent print. "This one's from a Paris label. They do a lot of printed styles—lovely, sophisticated colors."

The customer reached a hand out from behind the curtain and grabbed the clothes hanger, pulling the dress into the fitting room. There was lengthy rustling as she got changed. I wondered whether I should go do something else, but I decided to wait. Store policy is that the same member of staff stays with a customer for the duration of their visit. Many of our clothes can be somewhat challenging to work into a look, so we pride ourselves on helping customers find the style that works best for them.

To do this, you really have to start by knowing what your customer is like. What age are they? How tall? What about their personality? As it was, this customer had come in just as I was serving one of our regulars a cup of English tea, so all I'd seen was her hand as she pulled the curtain closed, saying, "I'm trying this on."

"What sort of size would you normally take in a dress, madam?"

"I forget. Hard to keep track."

Perhaps she was extremely shy, and it had taken all her courage to come in to our boutique after seeing us featured in some magazine. And then maybe she still couldn't bear for us to see her, because of her insecurities about her height or her weight, and had missed her opportunity to safely leave the booth.

"Do you tend to choose a trouser look, madam, or would you more often wear a skirt?"

"Sometimes I more often wear a skirt, and sometimes I tend toward a trouser."

Another possibility was that she'd recently had plastic surgery, and her face had collapsed while she was getting changed. She might be desperately adjusting silicone at this very moment. When I was younger, I heard about a woman who'd disappeared from a fitting room while on vacation overseas. There was a trapdoor in the floor of the booth, and she'd been sold straight to people smugglers. Maybe I could scare my customer into leaving the fitting room by telling her that story. That might actually be good customer service—less likely to cause offense than saying, "Please do feel free to step out and look in this larger mirror here!"

"Are you on your way home from work today?"

"Does that have anything to do with finding something to wear?"

Or what if it was a woman who'd once been humiliated in a fitting room, trying to take revenge on retail staff by haunting us? I nearly freeze whenever I'm walking down a street at night and hear the sound of high heels behind me. It must be the guilt from constantly telling customers, "Lovely!" or, "Oh, that suits you so well," regardless of what they try on.

She was still in there at 8:00 p.m.—closing time. I checked in with her several times, to no avail. I could hardly draw the curtains myself, so I had no choice but to say, "There's no rush, madam," and settle in. The customer kept making rustling sounds inside the booth, and once in a while I'd hear her murmur, "Oh, my!" or "Hrm-mm." She requested each piece in every size and color, one after the other. Barreling around our storeroom to gather all the items she asked for, I wondered what her story was, what important occasion she might be shopping for with such thoroughness. I asked my manager for the keys to the store. I'd made up my mind to stay after everyone else went home, to help my customer find what she was looking for. Our regulars could count on their favorite member of staff to be at their service at any time with just a phone call, so we often stayed open after hours for a single customer.

By the time the clock rounded midnight, my customer had finished trying on every piece of clothing in the shop. Which would she choose? I made a cup of tea and set it by the sofas for when she finally emerged. But it wasn't to be—she didn't come out of the fitting room, dressed in the clothes she'd arrived in. Instead, she called out that she wanted to go back to the very first thing she'd tried on. Then, she wanted to do the same with every single piece in the shop. My stamina finally gave out around 3:00 a.m.

In the morning, when I woke up on the shop sofa, the customer was still in the fitting room. She'd been trying to find something to wear all night. Poor, awkward lamb! I was starting to have a soft spot for her. I decided to run out to a local bakery that opened at six, and placed the bagel and the café au lait I'd bought just outside the curtain, saying, "Please, help yourself." She didn't respond, but the paper bag was gone when I next looked.

I touched up my makeup and changed into some spare clothes I had in my locker before the other staff arrived. "It's not your customer from yesterday, is it?" they said, surprised, but thankfully, when I said, "I know! She asked me to open up first thing," they didn't probe any further. By midafternoon, she'd completed her second try-on of all the clothes I'd brought out from stock. Still, she wasn't satisfied. I drove to the nearest fast-fashion outlet and purchased dozens of pieces for her. Some other customers came to our boutique, but I left them to my colleagues to serve. There were two other fitting rooms, so no one seemed to notice my peculiar customer.

She didn't like any of the clothes I'd bought for her either, so finally I decided to take her to another clothes shop, fitting room and all. I'd just remembered that our owner liked to change the decor of the boutique every once in a while, so our fitting rooms were movable, on wheels.

"Tell everyone I'll be out for a bit," I said to one of the other girls, and hooked the rope around my shoulders. It was heavy, but

(*my peculiar customer*)

attach rope here . . .

ここにともをつけると…

引っぱれる！！

. . . and pull!!

not impossible to pull forward. I headed into town, towing the fitting room. Pulling a thing like this in broad daylight, I'd been prepared for people to stare, but no one seemed to give it a second glance. I guess they thought we were setting up for some event or doing a photo shoot. My customer inside the booth, who'd been so hard to please, seemed to be having misgivings, saying, "There's no need for you to go to so much trouble."

"Please don't be silly. We've come so far—we're going to find the perfect thing for you, I promise," I said, trying to keep her spirits up. "I want you to come out of that fitting room with a smile on your face!"

I was set on finding my customer something really special. I thought I'd take her to my favorite boutique. That meant navigating a serious hill through steep residential streets. I called on passersby for help. "What's behind the curtain?" they wanted to know. When I said, "A valued customer," someone said, "That's a funny way of getting publicity," but several of them offered to help push to the top of the hill anyway.

Together, we transported the fitting room. The steeper the incline got, the more the curtains swayed, and gradually I was able to make out the shape of my customer inside. No one else seemed to be looking, but I could see she wasn't fat at all. She was smallish, but not especially tiny. More to the point, she didn't really seem human. Draped in the curtains, she was an unusual shape that I'd never seen before. From time to time I could hear a sticky, slurping, roiling kind of sound, and then the curtain would bulge and cave in different places. I had no idea what she was at all. But it was really no wonder she couldn't find an outfit that suited her when her body type was so unique!

I was just catching my breath, having towed the fitting room to the top of the hill—all that remained was to descend the hill on the other side—when the rope slipped from my hands and the fitting room started rolling down the steep street, casters rattling. I'd used up all my strength and didn't have the energy to run after it. The fitting room hurtled down toward the bottom of the hill at an incredible speed, growing smaller and smaller.

"Madam!" I cried, as loud as I could. "You're welcome to take that curtain, if you'd like."

A hand stuck out from between the curtains and waved slowly at me for a long time, like someone saying goodbye from a departing car window. Then the hand threw something into the road.

When I ran to pick it up, I saw it was a bank note in a currency I didn't recognize.

Since then, I've taken to imagining all sorts of things about the things I see as I walk down the street. Anything at all could turn out to be something beyond my wildest dreams. My customer's physique was kind of runny and grotesque, but depending on how you looked at it, you could also call it elegant. Picture a picnic blanket laid on a meadow—I bet that would look pretty good on her, like a floral print dress.

Typhoon

"TRY THESE—THEY'RE REALLY DELICIOUS."

I was in the bus shelter opposite the train station, staying out of the rain while I waited for my mom, when the old guy holding the umbrella and dressed in rags started talking to me. I hadn't noticed him turn up, but he gave me a friendly smile and offered me a little packet of cookies.

"You look hungry," he said. "Go ahead, take some."

Even though we were in the middle of a huge typhoon and

the ferocious wind was howling past my ears, I thought I caught a whiff of the old guy's sour smell.

"Aw, cookies!" I said, taking them like a good child.

I was clutching the cookies inside my palm and nervously pretending to eat them when the guy pointed toward the junction where the wide station road met a smaller road and, out of nowhere, said, "Don't ever underestimate people like them." He was pointing at a man in a suit waiting for the lights to turn, desperately holding his umbrella open in the storm.

I didn't react, but secretly I was pretty worried that he'd read my mind. I'd been watching people just like suit man passing by, laughing at them inside. Anytime I saw typhoon coverage on TV, I just had to wonder: What on earth were these people thinking? Walking along looking totally focused on holding their umbrellas open in front of them when their clothes, their hair, and most likely even their socks were wet through. I wanted to say, Are you sure there isn't something wrong with your head? Are you grown men really kowtowing to umbrellas? But I'd never mentioned these thoughts to anyone else.

"Just watch," said the old guy. "Soon he'll be down to bare bones."

I didn't know what he meant, but his voice was strong like a sea captain's, so I looked to where his gnarly finger was pointing, at the man in a suit holding on for dear life to the guardrail by the crossing. I'd nearly been blown out onto the road there too, earlier, as I battled the rain that blew horizontally into my face. Because it was a junction, the strong winds bore straight at you.

"Three! Two! One!" the old guy shouted, just as the man's umbrella turned inside out like a rice bowl and its fabric disappeared as though an invisible man had ripped it off, instantly reducing the umbrella to just its skeleton.

I was speechless. The old guy's timing had been perfect.

Associating with people like him was a bad idea. I knew this, but his shabby appearance and offensive smell didn't bother me anymore. He handed me another packet of cookies, and I pretended to nibble them again, apologizing to him in my head for deceiving him. Oblivious to that, the guy started telling a story about some boy from a tribe that lived deep in a forest. He was explaining what the young kid did to win an umbrella that a foreigner had brought to their village.

"They beat each other with sticks," said the guy. The wind was whipping his long, tangled hair around, and it looked like the strands were trying to feed on his face.

"Sticks?" I said.

"That's right. In that village, they had a custom: once a year, the men would take turns hitting each other with a tree branch. So the village chief decided that whoever lasted the longest before letting out even a single sound would win the umbrella. None of the villagers had any idea what the umbrella was for. They thought the foreigners must use it to hit each other, as they did with sticks. No one in the village wanted to avoid getting rained on. Local tradition had it that rain was caused by sylvan spirits and was essential to the villagers' reincarnation as insects after their death. People get reborn as insects in their mythology."

Something unpleasant crawled up my spine, as if I'd just looked at a cluster of something tiny all packed together, like bug eggs. As soon as the guy had said "sylvan spirits," I'd suddenly felt fearful and panicked about standing there next to him. Had I gotten myself into some kind of unsavory situation? I couldn't take my eyes off the tip of the umbrella he was gripping. I stuffed the cookies he'd given me into a pocket.

The guy was still talking, his hair still nibbling away at his face. "The young boy wanted the umbrella so badly that he became the first boy ever to take part in the village custom of the men hitting each other with sticks. His opponent kept hitting him and hitting him, but he stuck it out to the end without uttering a single peep. Young boy—not a single peep. Got that? When his towering opponent finally gave a groan at the pain in his arm and conceded, the boy collapsed, and lay still. That's right: he was dead.

"Can you guess why that young boy wanted the umbrella so badly?"

At the sudden question, I shook my head, and said, "Um, no, sir, I don't know."

"He believed that umbrellas could make you fly."

I was relieved that the story seemed to be over, but at the same time I was a little bit disappointed. Somehow, I'd been hoping for a more inspired ending. I was starting to wonder where my mom was, and about possible ways to safely remove myself from this conversation, when the guy pointed to another drenched man desperately holding his umbrella open. "They still believe too." Then he counted, "Three! Two! One!" like before—and I couldn't believe my eyes.

The man, who'd been getting buffeted along, holding aloft his nearly closed umbrella, stepped onto the guardrail and spring-boarded off, catching the wind and soaring up high into the air.

"All right!" The old guy looked to the sky and pumped his fist. "He really committed, kept his center of gravity nice and low—I knew he had a good chance!"

I stuck my head out from the bus shelter and looked in the direction where the man in the suit had flown off. Wiping the hair and the rain out of my eyes as I scanned the sky, I spotted loads of tiny human figures floating among the dark clouds. I stared, mouth wide open. All of them were hanging on for dear life, writhing and flailing, trying to keep a grip on their umbrellas. Fifty of them, at least, or a hundred, or even more.

I could have sworn the old guy was still right behind me, but when I snapped out of it and turned around, he was nowhere to be seen. Or at least he wasn't in the bus shelter anymore.

"Catch ya later!" I heard a voice say from above. It was the guy, sounding exultant. "Catchyalater! Catchyaaa! Laterrr!"

I don't laugh anymore when the news shows drenched people whose umbrellas flip and turn to bones. I don't belittle their mental capabilities. When I pass people on the street who insist on trying to hold their umbrellas open on a stormy day, I know they are far more attuned to things than I am, that they're fearless and dreaming big. And if I ever meet a boy looking cynical during a typhoon while sheltering from the rain, I'll be ready to offer him some cookies and say, "Try these. They're really delicious."

On my way home from the bus stop, I gingerly tasted one of the cookies he'd given me. It was crisp and delicate, and better than any other cookie I'd had in all my eleven years.

The old guy was found on the pavement all flattened out the next day, but I still tell this story anytime I'm out drinking and need something to entertain the group. If I tell it right, the part that goes, "Catchyalater! Catchyaaa! Laterrr!" is always a real crowd-pleaser.

I Called You by Name

ALL THROUGH THE MEETING, I WAS SO DIS-tracted by the bulge in the curtain I could hardly sit still.

Why wasn't it bothering anyone else? The light green drape pooled so unnaturally at the side of the window. No generous depth of pleating could cause a bulge like that. We were seated around three sides of a table, and I was the only one directly opposite the bulge. No matter how many times I told myself to forget it, no matter how hard I tried to concentrate on the discussion, the curtains came into my sight every time I looked up, and there was just no way I could focus on my team's proposals.

Should I tell them? Maybe say, *Look, someone's in there*, make it sound like a joke. But I didn't know how; I hadn't established myself as the kind of person who could say that sort of thing. Plus, this was an important meeting for me. After more than six months of strategizing and ingratiating myself, I'd finally won the advertising contract for a major telecomm firm. I was staking my career on my promise to deliver on the client's request for an "eye-catching stunt that would get people talking." I had to focus. My team was all men, all younger than I was. If that bulge turned out to be nothing more than a swell in the drape, they'd decide they couldn't take me seriously. *Just a woman after all*, they'd think, even though I was better at the job than any of them.

The room was a big one. I hadn't been able to reserve any of the upstairs spaces, so we'd ended up in the conference room on the ground floor, which held forty people. The distance between me and the window was the length of four long tables, at least. That made me even less confident about what I was seeing.

The first member of my team finished presenting his idea. I said, "I see. Not bad, but don't you think it's a little . . . run-of-the-mill? Who's next?"

As soon as the next guy stood up to explain his idea, my attention was back on the drape. Perhaps the suspicious bulge was just a trick of the light and would disappear if I got up close to it. Perhaps I'd pulled too many all-nighters and was starting to hallucinate. Perhaps . . .

Yes, I'd always been easily frightened, ever since I was small. I was much more prone than the average person to experiencing pareidolic phenomena, which is when any grouping of three dots starts to look like a pair of eyes and a mouth. I'd see it every-where. Three wrinkles on a suit in my wardrobe would easily re-veal themselves to be a face, and I couldn't look at wood grain for longer than three seconds. It was only recently that I'd found out there was a name for this. It had come up as a question on a quiz show I was watching: "What is the name of the effect, often seen in photographs purporting to show ghosts and spirits, in which a set of three marks is perceived to be a human face?"

That probably explained it: Drapery Bulge Effect. I'd nearly convinced myself I was just imagining things, but then I thought I saw the bulge move. My mind went blank. There was definitely someone in there. I didn't know why, but they were hiding behind the drape.

I reached for my bottle of water to steady myself. The aware-ness that I was supposed to be chairing this meeting stopped me from crying out, but I was terrified by what I was seeing. Was it a criminal? A naked person? *Who are you?*

The second presenter sat down. I said, "Very interesting," and nodded, pointlessly stroking the cap on my bottle of water. For a moment there was a strange silence, and I worried that I'd said something odd, but then everyone started talking among themselves, and I calmed down a little too. I could probably afford to wait a little longer. If it came to it, as long as I was decisive in giving the evacuation order, my team and I could safely escape. I wanted to examine all the possibilities first, rather than bringing the situation to my team's attention prematurely.

"Who's next?"

I thought back to when I went to a furnishings store to look at curtains with my boyfriend, when we were planning on living together—my ex, whom I'd broken up with just last month, when I found out he was seeing someone else, even though we'd discussed getting married one day. Maybe some part of me wished that it was him hiding behind there, and this was making the bulge look tens of times bigger than it actually was.

Forget about all that, I told myself. Focus on the meeting. I tried to read my handout, but the memory of what had happened with my ex was bubbling up now. Screw the meeting. The truth was, I wouldn't be in this job if I had a choice. What I really wanted was to marry him, fill our place with meticulously selected antique-style furniture, and do housework for him all day long. I was confident in my ability to cook, clean, and launder to perfection. So why did you have to be walking down that street, of all streets, arm in arm with her? All you had to do was do it discreetly so I didn't find out. Or at least have the decency to come clean when I confronted you, instead of ghosting me! Was that how little I was worth? Not even worth dumping? Was I an old hag? I was so thankful that I'd managed to hold back from crying out when I first spotted the bulge in the curtain. If I had let out some kind of shriek, I probably would have had to fall to my knees out of sheer humiliation.

The third person finished presenting. I was beyond being able to come up with any appropriate feedback. I said, "Okay, time to discuss as a group."

My team seemed to be taken aback by my unexpected suggestion. "Right now? Don't you think we should hear all the proposals first?" they asked.

I cut them off, saying, "No, this'll do."

They could hardly keep complaining after that, so they all gathered around the whiteboard and started brainstorming. I was the only one who stayed seated, glaring directly at the curtain.

The main question is, Why on earth are your curves quite so suggestive? I lost my confidence there for a minute, but I refuse to accept for another instant that anything about you could be a figment of my imagination. It can't just be me—how many people all around the world have you bamboozled, all bloused out like this? Is there someone in there? Or isn't there? Make up your mind! I've wasted too much of my life waiting around for ambivalent beings like you. Ghosters. Men who let you down easy. You must think you're really something. Calling yourself a phenomenon. What's the big deal about three points looking like a face? Maybe this makes me sound over the hill. A girl as young as the one he was cheating on me with wouldn't give you a second thought. But I can't just forgive you, not when you're puffed up so suggestively. You have no idea what kind of effect you have on people around you. Do you understand the heartbreak of realizing you've lost the ability to respond to things you've seen with your very own eyes with genuine surprise? How it feels when rationality, and hard-won experience, and your career all suddenly seem pointless? How far I've strayed from the carefree, innocent child I was. All that youth, and the potential that I must have once had, wasted. When I look at you, I'm confronted by the fact that I've turned into a totally uninteresting person. Don't you dare make me remember who I used to be.

"You've got to be joking. A roomful of grown men put their heads together and this was all you could come up with? I can't believe you're actually getting paid for this shit."

Maybe it's like this. Sad people like me are on the rise because of numbskulls like you who blow up like balloons without a single thought for the consequences. You get all our hopes up. We think, *This time, this time, I'll find someone for sure.* But because you're never there, we have to learn to be pragmatic, explain things away rationally. Sure, there might be other things that teach us to do this, but the first betrayal each of us goes through is at the hands of a bulge in a curtain. At least it was that way for me. You were the very first to let me down. You imprinted me with some kind of habit for being betrayed. Men keep lying to me and abandoning me. No matter how devoted I am to them. You're where it all starts.

"Put down your markers this instant and eat some chocolate. Get your blood sugar up. Eat until you come up with some ideas."

Why don't you show yourself already? You can't possibly think people are going to keep looking for you forever? I was sick and tired of it all. I wanted to get to a world where there was only yes or no. Ones and zeros.

"Eat, then write. Squeeze some ideas out of your sorry brains. Get on it!"

When I looked again, the bulge in the curtain—unless it was my imagination?—had shrunk a little. Wait. You're leaving? Without a word? Just because I told you how I really felt? That's exactly what I mean when I say you're unfair. Wait a second. I didn't mean it. Don't go. I don't have the strength to make it through this life on my own. Why do you all try to leave me? You're not even there anyway, are you? Of course you aren't. In which case the least you can do before you go is listen to the story of my first time. I was in third grade when I first found you all swollen up. Upstairs, in my room. Just after lunchtime, during summer vacation. Both my parents were out. I was rearranging posters on the wall, trying out one unsatisfactory layout after another. At first I thought you were a trick of the light. When I came closer timidly and touched you, it even seemed like you got a little bigger, right there in front of my eyes. See, it's starting to come back to you, isn't it? Right away, I ran out to the garden and looked up to the second floor to check on you through the window. But there was no one inside. I even climbed out onto the roof, but it made no difference—I still couldn't see anyone.

I was scared at first, but I also sensed that you were a presence that would protect me, so I let you stay. You lived with me for twenty days. I got to know you enough to wish you sweet dreams every night, and since I couldn't use my curtains, I set up a cardboard box to keep the sunrise from disturbing us. Huh, I guess I was already desperate to make people stay, even back then.

Our parting came suddenly. One day, I went into my room to find the edge of the curtain, which I'd carefully tied back, undone, and the curtains firmly closed. It was my own fault, for keeping our relationship a secret from my mother. I rushed to open them, in tears, thinking you'd left me without even a word. We'd spent twenty days together, but there was no one there. Just the lace curtain puddled in the corner, like a shell you'd discarded. I called out your name. That's right. I'd given you a name.

Never mind. It's too painful remembering the way I used to be. Back then I never bothered with boring explanations. My mind was open to anything. I wasn't worried about being disrespected by my team, or of people thinking I was a crazy woman. I didn't let myself be bound by anything as common as common sense.

I looked at the whiteboard and saw the colorful ideas that my men had scrawled onto it, all overlapping each other. There was no way I could decipher who had written what. Ugh. Were they all idiots? Feeling that I'd just remembered something precious, I drew three black dots on the back of my handout, and chuckled.

∵

"Hey, come look at this. It looks like a face, even though all I did was go dot, dot, dot!"

My team leaned in and peered at the sheet.

"Is everything okay, boss?"

"Are you feeling all right?"

I got out of my chair, gave them a cute little wave when I reached the door, and put the conference room behind me. I skipped down the long tiled walkway we complained about having to walk down in heels to go buy lunch, and broke into a sprint, rounding a corner shouting, "*Ch-ch-chaaaaaaaaaarge!*" I looked over my shoulder and there, on the face of a high-rise, I saw three yellow window-cleaning platforms suspended in midair. When I realized they were positioned precisely like those three points I'd drawn earlier, I nearly peed myself. I knew that someone—someone very big—had found me. *It's about time you finally turned up*, I said to him as the tears rolled down my face.

An Exotic Marriage

ONE DAY, I REALIZED THAT I WAS STARTING TO look just like my husband.

It wasn't that someone pointed it out. It occurred to me by accident, while I was sorting through some files that had accumulated on the computer, comparing photos from five years ago, before we were married, to more recent ones. I couldn't have described how, exactly. But the more I looked, the more it seemed as if my husband was becoming similar to me, and me to him.

"The two of you? I can't say I've noticed it," my brother, Senta, said when I mentioned it. I had called him to get help with the computer. He spoke in his usual slow way, like a languid animal resting by water. "You must have just adopted each other's expressions from spending a lot of time together."

"By that logic, you and Hakone should look even more alike," I said, double-clicking on a folder as he'd instructed.

Senta and his girlfriend, Hakone, had started dating in their teens, so they'd been together twice as long as my husband and I. We'd gotten married a year and a half after we met.

"Being married must be different from just living together," he said.

"Different how?"

"Dunno. More . . . concentrated?"

Senta directed me to drag the folder containing the photos over to the icon of the camera.

"I've done this before," I said. "Every time I try, it goes *boinng!* right back to where it came from."

As expected, I had to contend with the *boinng!* at least twice, but eventually managed to back up the photos. I told him we were thinking of selling our refrigerator on an online auction site soon and asked him to think of any tips, and then we hung up.

I took a package to the post office for my husband. On the way back, I saw Miss Kitae sitting on a bench inside the dog run. When I knocked on the glass, she looked up and beckoned to me, so I decided to stop in for a minute.

Our apartment complex had a private dog run. It was a small park that had been created by decking over the top of the roof that extended over the entrance, and could be accessed from the hallway on the second floor. I pushed open the heavy steel fire door.

"San, dear, over here," Kitae said, patting the empty space next to her on the bench. "Visit with me for a bit. I know you're not busy."

She pulled her customized shopping cart toward her and passed me a canned coffee from the rear pocket. Her beloved cat, Sansho, was on a string leash and curled up on a cushion on top of the cart like a piece of decor, as usual. Kitae brought Sansho out to sun in the dog run every day after lunch, saying it was only fair, since she paid the same rent as our neighbors who had dogs. Kitae was nearly thirty years older than I was, but she exuded health and had a marvelously straight back. Her skin was so dewy she could have easily been mistaken for someone in her fifties, if not for her gray hair. She pulled off white jeans better than I could ever hope to.

I had first met her in the waiting room at the veterinary clinic I took my cat to, where she'd confided in me at length about Sansho's toilet problems. Our apartment complex was a large one, unusual for the area, with two wings, a west wing and an east wing. The resident turnover was quite high, and most of us didn't socialize with our neighbors. Kitae was probably the only one I could claim to know. At first, I'd kept some distance from her strange habit of dragging her cat outside against its will, but as she kept greeting me, I gradually started to get to know her, partly out of interest in Sansho, who always lay unmoving on the cushion like a stone statue.

I sat down next to her and pulled up the tab on the canned coffee. "What a nice day," I said, even though the humidity was making my T-shirt cling damply to my skin.

"I can't stand the Japanese summer. So wet and miserable." Kitae looked across the sunny wooden deck and pulled an exaggerated grimace. Before moving here, she and her husband had lived in an apartment in San Francisco. She'd told me recently that they'd bought it when they were still young. When its value had skyrocketed, it had been good news—until their property taxes went up too, and they'd had no choice but to sell up and come back to Japan.

Really, San, it was five million yen a year, for an apartment we'd already paid for. Five million! What a joke!

I'd seen Kitae's husband around just once—my impression of him was of a gentle man smiling while he listened to Kitae talk, like a jizo statue, or Sansho.

Kitae asked after anything exciting going on in my life.

"I'm starting to look like my husband." I found myself telling her about the photos.

She stopped waving the hand she'd been using as a fan and said, "Dear me," displaying an unexpected level of interest. "Tell me again how long you've been married."

"Coming up to four years."

"Now, I could be wrong—I haven't known you long enough to say—but you should be careful. You're accommodating, San, and before you know it, girls like you get all—"

A corgi running around on the deck barked at a butterfly, and I missed the end of Kitae's sentence. I hoped she might repeat herself, but she was too busy lifting up her bangs with one hand while flapping the other to cool herself.

"Show me those photos next time," she said.

"I will."

Kitae pulled her cart over to scratch Sansho under his jaw. It seemed like a good time to leave, but then she took out an individually wrapped cookie from the rear pocket of the cart and started talking again.

"A married couple I know," she said, and I nodded and hurriedly sat my bottom back down firmly on the bench. Her story, which she told me while breaking the cookie into pieces, went like this.

There was once a husband and wife. Of course, Kitae knew their names and faces—they were old friends of her and her husband's. The two couples had socialized together, but after Kitae and her husband had moved to San Francisco, they didn't get the chance to meet again until nearly ten years later.

During those ten years, the other couple had moved to England. Kitae visited London and arranged to meet up with them. When she arrived at the restaurant, they stood up to greet her—"Long time no see!"—and Kitae was astounded at what she saw.

"They'd grown identical, like twins," she said, closing her eyes as though she were recalling the sight.

"Did they resemble each other to begin with?" I asked.

"That's the thing. They'd been nothing like each other. Which was why I wondered, just for an instant, whether they'd had plastic surgery."

During the meal, Kitae tried to compare the couple's faces, looking discreetly from one to the other. She considered that it might have been the result of their aging, but the degree to which they'd changed couldn't be put down solely to the effects of time. Plus, and this was very strange indeed, when she considered the individual features separately—eyes, noses, mouths—the two of them were clearly different people. But the moment she saw their faces as a whole, somehow they seemed like mirror images. Kitae felt uneasy, as though she were being duped.

"Was it the way they ate? Their mannerisms or their body language?" I accepted a piece of cookie.

She leaned her head to one side, thinking. "Maybe that was part of it. But it was more that there was something drawing them closer. As if they couldn't help but imitate each other." She frowned.

The even more surprising thing was that the wife was tucking happily into platters of oysters and lobster, which she'd disliked years ago. As far as Kitae could recall, it had only been the husband who'd had a fondness for those things. When she casually brought that up, the wife said, "What? Really?" and looked startled. After a while, she said, "That's not true. I've always loved oysters," and turned to her husband. "Isn't that right?"

Beside her, the husband nodded in agreement.

They finished their meal before Kitae's foggy doubts had cleared.

"We promised to see each other again soon, but then . . . ," she said, poking a piece of cookie toward Sansho's nose.

"It didn't work out that way?" I said.

"No," she said. "The next time we met was another ten years later."

Kitae turned up at the same restaurant, where they'd arranged to meet again, feeling a little nervous. When they stood up from their chairs and turned toward her, she exclaimed to herself in surprise. Even from a slight distance, she could see that they'd reverted to their original, un-like, separate selves.

"I felt almost cheated," Kitae said, munching a piece of cookie in which Sansho had shown no interest. "Because a part of me had been hoping they'd have become even more alike."

The three of them finished their meal and headed toward the main street to find a taxi. Kitae looked at the husband's back as he walked ahead and, suddenly feeling laughter bubbling up, turned to the wife and confessed what had been on her mind for the last ten years. "I don't know what got into me. I guess I imagined it."

The couple invited Kitae back to their place and drank wine until the husband passed out. After Kitae and the wife had emptied their third bottle, the wife said, "Kitae, darling, why don't we step out and have a look in the garden?"

Kitae had been gazing at the rocks that were placed around the house, thinking the display was in peculiar taste. She got up and followed the wife outside unsteadily. In the moonlight the wife made her way through the English-style garden and crossed a small bridge over the pond. Eventually, she stopped in front of a flower bed blooming with salvia.

"I'm going to let you in on a secret, about how I got back to the way I was," the wife said. It must have been the wine that made her sound like she was trying not to giggle.

"What are you talking about?" Kitae asked.

"I mean how I got back to myself. You'd like to know, wouldn't you? That's the secret," the wife said, and pointed to the side of the flower bed.

"A rock?" The moonlit flower bed was strewn with fist-size stones similar to the ones inside the house.

"Exactly. My stand-ins." The wife told Kitae to pick one up.

Doubtfully, Kitae crouched and chose one. Like the ones inside the house, it was a lumpy, thoroughly ordinary rock. "What about it?" Kitae asked, impatient.

"Look closer," the wife said. "You'll see that it's nearly a perfect likeness."

"Likeness? To what?"

"You'll see it. Just look."

Kitae stood up and looked at the rock in the moonlight. She half thought she was being played for some kind of joke, but when she changed the angle of the rock slightly, she felt her tipsiness evaporate.

"Incredible," she said softly. There was the nose, the eyes—the resemblance to the husband was remarkable.

"Isn't it?"

The wife explained that it had all started with the stones in the flower dish she'd put by their bedside. "They'd get to look so much like him, and I had to keep swapping them out. They just kind of piled up." Only then did Kitae notice that there were countless rocks of a similar size by the side of the salvia bed.

I let out a breath. "It reminds me of the story of the three talismans."

"How does that one go?" Kitae tilted her head to one side.

"Wasn't it about a monk who was nearly devoured by a mountain hag, and stuck a talisman on a pillar in the lavatory to take his place?"

Kitae said, "Right," though I couldn't tell whether she was interested or not. She got up, saying, "She asked me whether I wanted to take one as a souvenir, but I couldn't. It would have been just a little too peculiar, don't you think?"

Yukiko Motoya

We were the only ones left in the dog run. "Thank you for the coffee," I said, and rushed to open the fire door for Kitae, who had started pushing her cart toward it. I watched for a while as she made her way across the suspended walkway toward the east wing, and then made my way back to the west wing.

Back in the apartment, I picked up around the living room and switched on the Roomba.

What with the built-in dishwasher doing the dishes after breakfast, and the washing machine drying the laundry too, I sometimes got confused about who did the housework around here. Before I was married, I'd had an office job at a water cooler company. The company was small and understaffed, and when I met my future husband the workload was taking a toll on my health. I only found out his earnings were more than average after we started dating, but when he told me I shouldn't keep working if I didn't want to, I leapt at the opportunity. Since then, though I called myself a homemaker, I felt a lingering guilt about just how easy I had it. Owning a home at this age, I felt as if I'd somehow managed to cheat at life. I almost wished for a child so I could have a good reason to stay at home, but—perhaps because my motives were impure—there was no sign of us conceiving anytime soon.

It was past one o'clock. I remembered that it was the use-by date for the ground meat in the fridge, so I decided to fry it up with sweet chili miso and eggplant. My mind kept going back to the couple Kitae had talked about earlier. *Was it all true? What happened to them after that?* I couldn't get them out of my head. I tried to tell my husband the story when he came back from work, but somehow it didn't seem as mysterious or resonant as when Kitae told it.

"What is that, some kind of horror story?" My husband was picking pieces out of his miso soup, like a bird pecking at birdseed. I'd repeatedly asked him not to, but he claimed a doctor had told him to watch his salt intake, and since then he'd made a point of leaving the broth almost untouched every night.

I reached for the dish of green onions and cuttlefish tentacles in vinegar and miso dressing, and took the opportunity to look at my husband's profile as he sat at the table. Because he preferred to watch TV during dinner, my customary seat was on his right, side-on rather than across from him.

My husband was engrossed in some variety show, highball tumbler happily in hand. It was a habit he'd kept completely secret while we were dating. Soon after our wedding, he'd sat me down and said, "San, you should know that I'm a man who likes to watch at least three hours of TV a day."

I'd never been married before, but my husband had previously had a failed marriage. He said he'd hidden his bad habits from his first wife, trying to keep up appearances, and that had become too much of a burden. "That's why I want to show you the real me," he said. He'd sounded so sincere that I unthinkingly welcomed it as a good thing.

I discovered that night that "TV" meant variety shows. Nor was "three hours" an exaggeration—each night, for at least the time it took to have a drink and eat dinner, his attention was glued to the screen as though he were suckling it with his eyes. Having successfully exposed me to the "real" him, my husband eventually worked up to making it clear, every chance he got, that he was a man who liked to not think about anything when he got home.

I examined his features more closely. My husband's eyes were piercing, to put it nicely. To put it another way, they constantly looked suspicious, even reptilian. Because of his bad posture, he always looked as though he were peering up at the world, and eight or nine times out of ten, he gave people an unpleasant first impression. His nose was long, as though it had been pushed down from above, and his lips were thin.

My face, on the other hand, was pretty average. I had a round, low nose that took after my grandfather's. My lips, which were like my grandmother's, were plump, but thanks in part to the paleness of my skin, the overall impression was bland, so that sometimes even I looked in the mirror and was reminded of a blank postcard. What was more, my face lacked cohesion, because the right eyelid had one fold and the left had two. I'd had a boyfriend or two who'd told me they liked the way I looked, so I wasn't unhappy with my face, but now that I was married and had fewer reasons to put on makeup, my likeness to a blank postcard was perhaps more noticeable.

I couldn't imagine anyone thinking we resembled each other. So why had I felt that we did?

Out of nowhere, my husband said he wanted to go on a short vacation.

That day, my brother, Senta, had come around after work to repair the refrigerator he was going to post on an online auction for us. I had been watching him as he put down some sheets of newspaper, laid out the tools he'd brought, and tackled the task.

I turned toward my husband in the living room, surprised. "Where's this coming from?"

"I mean, we haven't gotten away in a while." My husband looked totally relaxed, highball in hand. We'd talked about order-ing in some pizzas once there was some progress on the repair, but he'd gone ahead and started drinking "to tide him over." He had no compunction about proclaiming that he had no interest in do-ing anything as tedious as rewiring household appliances. I guess he'd embraced his nature as the youngest of his siblings, because he showed no hesitation in taking advantage of kindness, even if it came from his younger brother-in-law.

Senta didn't help matters. He could have stood up for himself more, but there was something about him that almost volunteered for the position of junior partner. It went so far that, because my husband would call on him for every little thing, my brother and I saw a lot more of each other now than we had before I was married.

"San," my husband said from the couch, "do you remember Uwano? I brought him here once."

"The one who looks like a monkey? He put up that bookcase for us."

A few months after we'd been married, my husband had gotten it into his head that he wanted rows of shelves that went all the way up to the ceiling, and he had roped in his coworker to help. I guess he hadn't yet felt comfortable enough then to ask Senta.

"That's the one. Well, he says he just bought himself a brand-new camper van."

"He went for it, huh?"

"Yeah. But he's too busy to take it out."

"Right."

"So, you know, he says it's a pity to leave it lying around, and he just wants someone to enjoy it."

"Who's going to do that?"

"Me."

"Uwano doesn't want to drive it himself?"

"He's too busy. That's why we decided I should take it out instead. Weren't you listening to a word I said?"

"Can just anyone drive a camper van?"

"I guess so," my husband said.

"Senta, do you know if that's true?" I asked.

"I think all you need is a regular driver's license," he answered, working a fine brush that looked like a nail polish applicator. After multiple coats, the specialized adhesive would build up so that the repair would be undetectable to the untrained eye.

Last week, when I'd checked over the refrigerator to see whether we'd be able to sell it, I'd discovered two cracks in the seal around the door. Senta had told me they were fixable, so I'd asked him to do it. Now, seeing the way he knowledgeably laid out the professional-looking tools for the job, I couldn't help but think, as his older sister, that he should be training as some kind of craftsman instead of trying to make it as a film director.

"How many people can it take?"

"It's a six-seater. It even has a toilet and a shower," my husband said proudly, as though the van were his own. "So I was thinking, if you like, Senta, why don't you and Hakone come along too? There's enough space."

"Wow—really? I'll just check with Hakone," Senta said.

It was obvious he was trying to rope in Senta to take care of the parts of camping he didn't want to bother with.

"Great! I think we should head for the mountains, you know?"

"Are you thinking you'd bring the grill?"

"Of course. We'll put up hammocks, take it easy. Have some beers."

Once they'd enthusiastically painted this manly picture, Senta said he'd finished covering the cracks in white paint and was going to wait for it to dry. We ordered pizza.

"I don't know why, but I've been feeling drawn to the mountains lately. To nature," said my husband, who'd been rooted to the couch the entire time. "Just all of a sudden. I don't know what's gotten into me."

I recalled that the last time we'd been in a bookstore, he had in fact glanced through a field guide to wild plants.

"Sounds like you've been working too hard," Senta said.

"Right. Could be."

"Have you been putting in overtime?"

"Overtime? Yeah, I have." My husband was licking cheese off his fingers while nodding.

"What is it you want to do in the mountains?" Senta asked, sipping his cola.

"I really don't want to do anything. Just relax, zone out."

"Isn't it something?" I said, reaching for a slice of the quattro formaggi. "No one would guess this was the same guy who couldn't make enough fun of outdoorsy people just a little while ago."

"Maybe it's a midlife thing. Remind me how old you are now?"

"How old am I now again?" My husband turned his bulging eyes toward me.

"Why don't you know your own age?"

"I can't be bothered to work it out every time. This is why you need to remember things like this for me." Having said everything he wanted to say, and apparently eaten his fill, my husband went off to take a bath.

Senta polished off the remaining pizza, including what my husband had left, and went back to work on the refrigerator. I halfheartedly started moving the plates to the dishwasher.

It was the beginning of July.

I'd thought this would finally mean the end of the rainy season, but the humidity only rose, joining forces with the heat, and the weather became even more uncomfortable.

Unusually, my husband, who'd planned to go in to work over the weekend, said he had canceled and invited me to go out for food.

We were on our way back from a local lunch place, where we'd eaten a plate of soba noodles with grated daikon and yam, and a chicken-omelette rice bowl. Three things happened more or less at the same time. My husband, who'd been walking swiftly ahead, said, "Oh," and stopped short; a woman who'd been crouched down by a utility pole said, "Why!" and stood up; and, from my vantage point behind the two of them, I had a nasty premonition. I suspected my husband had been caught trying to spit out phlegm by the side of the road, as he had a habit of doing. I nervously approached them, and saw the woman was holding a dustpan and a brush. Her expression was thunderous, beyond what I'd expected, and I was considering walking past as though I had nothing to do with the situation when my husband, turning around, appealed to me for help. "San, can't you do something?"

"What happened?"

"Just get over here."

Hesitantly, I joined him and the woman, who was watching him sharply from behind her glasses. She looked about halfway between me and my mother in age.

"This woman," said my husband helplessly, still standing right in front of her, "even though I've explained that I didn't, she insists that I looked right at her and spat on the ground. You can set her straight, right? Tell her I'd never do something like that?"

"You think I couldn't see from this close?" the woman said. "Knock it off."

My husband had apparently decided to keep talking to me instead of her. "This is exactly the kind of thing I can't handle." He massaged the bridge of his nose with his fingers, looking genuinely pained. "Look, just tell her I feel bad about the spitting, okay?"

"Um," I started, before the woman could open her mouth. I chose my words carefully to sound as polite as possible. "People often misunderstand him—because of the way he looks—but he's not the kind of person to spit at someone deliberately."

"How should I know?" The woman's expression had grown even more ominous, as though she were trying to squash my husband's reptile eyes through the power of her gaze. "I assume you're married. You ought to be ashamed of yourselves, acting like this, and at your age." She looked at us closely from head to toe.

My husband was staring off over the woman's head. I looked down at my feet, unable to meet her eyes.

"Where do you live?" she asked.

I told her it was nearby, and the woman grimaced even more. "Give me the address," she said.

"Our address?" I raised my head in surprise. I didn't understand how that was relevant.

"Of course. It's only fair, since you know where I live. There's no telling what people like you will stoop to otherwise," she said loudly.

"Really," I said, entreating, "I assure you, it won't happen again." I bowed my head, desperately trying to bring a peaceful end to the situation. But when I looked to my husband, he'd quietly moved himself over to the shade of the boundary wall and was decidedly in spectator mode, as though he were watching TV.

"What do you think you're doing, trying to sneak away over there?" The woman's anger seemed to have reached a climax. She put her dustpan and brush down on the ground. "I've had enough," she said, and took her phone out of her pocket. "I'm calling the police."

"Wait, please. Let me clean it up," I said, pulling a handkerchief out of my bag and crouching down to the ground. Under the searing sun, the asphalt was as hot as a frying pan over low heat. I found the remains of a gob of phlegm to the side of the utility pole, and wiped it off carefully, collecting it in my handkerchief, then rubbed at the spot repeatedly.

I got up and bowed my head deeply again, asking her to accept my apology. When I raised my head, the woman was staring at me with a blank expression. Flustered by the change in the quality of her gaze, I bowed and apologized yet again. But the woman still wouldn't respond.

Wasn't this enough? I was considering getting back down and scouring the area again when the woman quietly said, "Look at yourself. It wasn't even yours."

I still wasn't sure what she meant. She picked up the dustpan and brush. "I'm done with this. Leave it. But don't come past my house again," the woman commanded, and then shooed us as if she were chasing away some animal.

My husband had started to walk away. I rushed around the corner after him.

"What a disaster," my husband said, as though he'd had nothing to do with it. "The old cow had it in for you. Bad luck."

I looked down at the handkerchief I was still holding in my hand. I had the strange sensation that my body was tangled with my husband's, or maybe cleaved to it. Until the woman had pointed it out, I had been feeling that the phlegm wrapped in the handkerchief belonged to me.

I looked over at my dawdling husband.

"Oh!" I exclaimed before I could stop myself.

My husband's features seemed to have slipped down his face toward his chin.

Then, as though reacting to my voice, they hurriedly moved back to their original position.

"What's the matter, San?" Surprised at my surprise, my husband peered at me. His face was his usual, somehow fishlike face. "What just happened?"

For a long moment I was speechless. Eventually my husband seemed to get bored, and said, "You know, you're starting to show your age, San." Then he ambled around the corner and disappeared.

When I paid careful attention, I could see that my husband's face changed nimbly in response to whatever situation he was in. When we were with people, it stayed looking the way it always looked, keeping up appearances, but once it was just the two of us, the position of his eyes and nose would take on a slightly haphazard placement. The difference was a millimeter or two, an indeterminate change, like the outline of a caricature dissolving and spreading in water.

I started finding excuses to make him look in the mirror when his face was slacking. *Hey, you missed a spot shaving,* I'd say, or, *You should check out that thing by your nose.* The moment he faced the mirror, his features, which had been sitting in approximate positions, would snap back into their original arrangement, as if they were lining up for inspection. At first I thought it was creepy, but seeing it every day, I started getting used to it, even finding it impressive.

The only time it still threw me off was when my husband's features would imitate mine. I assumed it did this because it saved effort to draw on a face that was close at hand. Either way, I noticed a clear pattern in that his features were most likely to become careless while he was watching a variety show with his nightly highball.

I was on my laptop at the dinner table, fresh from a bath, when my husband started talking about how his ex-wife was acting strange.

I finished my nightly survey of potential rival refrigerators up for auction, and closed the laptop.

"How do you mean, strange?"

I'd never asked him not to talk to her, and I'd had an inkling they'd been in contact, but it was the first time he'd brought her up so openly. Before we were married, he'd told me his ex-wife was happily with another man.

"She keeps sending me weird emails," my husband said, during the next ad break. Over the back of the couch I could see his upper back, which was starting to get fleshy, and the short hair covering the back of his head. This was the one he'd split up with after only two years because he'd gotten tired of not being able to be himself with her. That was definitely different, I thought, than leaving someone because you stopped being attracted to them.

"How are they weird?" I stood up and went to the kitchen to get the barley tea I'd brewed during the day.

"I don't even know how to describe them."

"But you said strange. What makes you say that?"

"They're kind of garbled, I guess."

"Are you going to reply?" I said.

"I already did." He was doing something with the TV remote. He said he'd written her back with vague generalities, and she'd responded with an even more incomprehensible message.

"Do you think she wants to get back together with you?" I asked blandly.

My husband said nothing.

Was his face staying in line just now, when he was thinking about his ex-wife? I wondered vaguely as I drank the cold barley tea. Another variety show came on.

I left the apartment to go to the dry cleaner's and spotted Kitae sitting on the bench in the dog run. She was sitting with her spine straight, neck long as usual, but her back seemed to be missing some of its usual vitality.

I leaned against the fire door and pushed it open to enter the dog run, and she waved at me quietly.

"No Sansho today?" I said, noticing that the ever-present polka-dotted cart was nowhere to be seen.

"No Sansho," Kitae said distractedly. She looked over to a brown dog that was trying to climb the fence. Normally, she would have insisted I sit down and keep her company. I waited a little, wondering if something was wrong, but she didn't say anything more.

The sun was nearly directly overhead. The light, which spent the morning thwarted by the apartment building, would soon overcome it and blaze triumphantly down onto the bench. Picturing Kitae's perfectly pale hair frizzling under its rays, I didn't feel right just leaving, and asked her, "Would you like to go to a café?"

Am I overstepping? Until now, we'd only met at the vet and the dog run. For a moment I worried, but Kitae glanced up with a look of mild surprise and said, "Sure. Let's go. There's a place I know near here that does a good red-bean shaved ice." With that, she started walking with powerful steps that belied her age.

We headed for a café off the main shopping street. It was an old-fashioned establishment with sooty lace curtains in the window. Kitae sat down at a corner table, took out a white terrycloth handkerchief from her pocket, and wiped her brow. "You know, I feel like a neapolitan spaghetti. Won't you have a bite to eat too?"

I decided to follow her recommendation of a red-bean shaved ice. I'd just had egg-and-lettuce fried rice for lunch.

It seemed presumptuous to ask whether something had happened, so I picked at the shaved ice for a while, listening to the sound of the TV filtering out from behind the counter, until Kitae abruptly stopped stirring her glass of water with her fork.

"Don't think me heartless," she said. When she saw I was at a loss as to how to respond, she continued, "I'm sorry, that's a lie. I'd rather you did think so."

Either way, I thought, *this doesn't sound like a conversation to be taken lightly.* "Of course, no, neither of those," I said, dismantling the mound of ice with my spoon.

"It's about Sansho," Kitae started, looking down at the neapolitan spaghetti the server had brought over. "His accidents just wouldn't clear up."

If I remembered right, it had been midsummer last year that the accidents had started. Kitae had been going to the vet with this problem for almost a whole year.

"I took him around to all the best clinics, but nothing seemed to help." Kitae let out a sigh as she reached for the grated cheese.

Our cat, Zoromi, had also gone through a phase of peeing outside her litter box when she'd first arrived as a kitten, perhaps as a form of protest at having been separated from her mother. The smell of cat urine had been overwhelming, and no amount of scrubbing with cleaner would get rid of it. What was more, once a spot on the rug was marked with her pee, Zoromi kept using the same spot. It was an expensive rug we'd invested in right after we got married, but, exhausted by the strain of repeatedly taking it in for dry cleaning, we'd tearfully evicted it from the apartment.

While our issue had resolved in about a month, when I thought of the despair I felt, wondering whether we'd be locked in the urine battle forever, I still broke out in a sweat. Because I hadn't heard any more about Sansho's problem, I'd assumed it had cleared up too.

But Kitae had been dealing with it all this time. Half admiringly, I asked, "So how is it now?"

It must have been the strain of having kept quiet about it for nearly a year: the lid popped off Kitae's mouth like a cork shooting out of a bottle.

"I thought I was going to have a breakdown. I know you had your rug issue, but Sansho started in the hallway just inside our entrance. In the beginning I looked on the bright side, thinking at least laminate was easy to clean. But he kept going in the same corner, and eventually it soaked into the wood. The smell got worse, and after a while I had to tape up a litter pad there where the wall met the floor. It was no time to worry about appearances, I tell you."

Having said that much without stopping for breath, Kitae finally let go of the canister of grated cheese she'd been clutching.

A thick layer of cheese had settled on her spaghetti, like the aftermath of a major snowfall.

"But that was only the beginning," she continued. "Maybe it never would have happened if I hadn't interfered."

Feeling, perhaps, that he'd been deprived of his chosen spot, Sansho started to go to the toilet on anything and everything fabric in the apartment. He went around deliberately marking cushions, laundry, the couch, and even the bed where Kitae and her husband slept. The two of them tried every tactic suggested by the vets, but nothing worked. They upholstered the sofa and the bed in litter pads and packing tape. They even covered their comforter and their pillows. As a result, there was an unpleasant rustling sound when they tried to sleep. At one point, they tried confining Sansho to his cat carrier. But he kept up such a piteous cry you'd have thought he was watching his mother die, and Kitae couldn't stand it. That was when an acquaintance mentioned that a change of scenery had cured their cat of the same problem. Kitae had started taking Sansho outside as though clinging to a lifeline.

"Do you know how many litter boxes we have around the apartment right now, San?" Kitae said, watching the back of the bored-looking waitress who'd just topped up our water. "Thirteen. Thirteen! I don't know anymore whether the cat lives with us or if we're the ones staying in the cat's bathroom!"

Kitae laughed. I still didn't know what to say, so I just kept on ferrying the red beans one by one to my mouth. Her whole situation seemed like a muddy bog where struggling would only get you sucked in deeper.

"What are you going to do?" I asked.

"We've had to decide to let him go." Of course, they would have preferred to find him another home, but there was no way someone would take him. They considered leaving him in the grounds of a shrine, but it seemed unlikely that Sansho, at nearly eleven, could start over as a stray. They'd searched and searched for a solution, until Kitae had stopped being able to eat.

That explains why I haven't seen her for a while, I thought.

"Which was why we thought of the mountains."

"The mountains?" I said.

There were tears in Kitae's eyes. "Yes, we thought the mountains, that could work."

Having said that much, Kitae finally started on her untouched neapolitan spaghetti. I realized I'd grown quite chilly because of the red-bean ice, and asked the server, who was watching TV behind the counter, to turn down the AC. I glanced at Kitae, who looked like a shrunken balloon, gazing down at her spaghetti and moving her fork obscurely in the noodles.

For our honeymoon, we'd gone to the Andes.

My husband, who had happened to see a clip of Machu Picchu

on TV while we were deciding on our destination, had suggested we might as well take the opportunity to go to South America.

With no background knowledge whatsoever, we'd signed up for a package tour recommended by the travel agent. I only found out after we'd paid the fee that Machu Picchu was a historic ruin of an ancient city that came into view atop a cliff at an altitude of approximately 2,400 meters above sea level. To get there, we'd have to take a plane, a bus, a train, and then another bus. It wasn't a trip to be taken lightly. Every informational website I checked emphasized the importance of making sure we were physically prepared for the rigors of what would be a demanding route.

We decided to start taking nightly walks to build up our stamina. But my husband would stop after a thirty-minute circuit of the local park, saying he'd had enough.

"If it comes to it, San, I'll just rest at the hotel, and you can record it all on video for me," he said.

But to my surprise, once we were in Cusco, while other members of the tour went down one after the other with altitude sickness, my husband alone walked around as if he'd sprouted wings on his back. I held my breath, thinking he was overdoing it and would crash later in the trip, but the next day, when we reached Machu Picchu, he said, "I feel a lot stronger than usual," and continued exploring the ruins with even more spring in his step.

"I guess I just needed more altitude this whole time," he said once we were back in Lima, the capital. While the other tourists, having recovered from the thinner air, were out making the most of an hour of free time, my husband reverted to his usual self and refused to even acknowledge the possibility of getting up from his seat at Starbucks. That was the memory that came to mind when Kitae mentioned mountains.

A few days later, my friend Hasebo, whom I'd known since high school, asked me to organize the after-party for her upcoming wedding. At first I demurred, saying there must be someone better for the job, but she said I seemed like the one with the most spare time to plan, which was true, so I agreed. For a while my days were as busy as back when I'd had my office job, and before I knew it the rainy season had given way to high summer.

"Look at you go," my husband would say every time he noticed me rushing around with party preparations in the blazing heat. "I can't believe you said yes. I wouldn't do it if you paid me."

"What else could I do? It's Hasebo," I said, feeling offended. He'd obviously forgotten how much she had done for us at our wedding.

"Hasebo—she was married before, right, already has kids? Then what difference does it make? Why are they even bothering with a wedding?"

"That's why they're doing the reception with family only, and all their friends are invited to the after-party," I said, recalling how I'd taken charge of most of the preparations for our wedding too.

"Make sure you get her to pay you, if it turns out to be too much work," he said, and without waiting for a response to this piece of totally unreasonable advice, turned back to the TV.

Each time I looked at my husband lying on the couch, I had the strange impression I was living with a new kind of organism that would die if it exerted itself in any way. Even when I told him about Sansho's toilet accidents, his only response was to pick up Zoromi from the floor and say, "Zoromi! *You're* not going to cause me any extra trouble, are you? Do you understand what I'm saying?"

How was it that he could have so little compunction about always letting someone else pick up the slack? I wanted to ask, but no doubt this exotic creature would consider the question just another thing that was too much effort to deal with. How had I ended up married to a completely different species of being from me?

I'd seen Kitae in the dog run several times since our last conversation, but between being short of time and feeling hesitant, I hadn't gone over to talk to her.

Do you really think Sansho's going to make it in the mountains? I'd almost said this to her as we stepped out of the café when we last met. But just before I could, my lips had crumbled and instead

I'd said, "I'll try the neapolitan next time," and on that irrelevant note we'd gone our separate ways. I resolved to ask her the next time we talked, but at the same time I also expected I wouldn't be able to, and those two feelings had hung suspended in the air ever since.

I was on my way back from a big stationery store in Shinjuku where I'd acquired supplies of construction paper and self-adhesive vinyl sheets for the after-party when I remembered that the dental clinic where Hakone worked was nearby. I decided to drop in. I hadn't had a chance to thank her properly for her and Senta's help selling the refrigerator.

As I went down the steps leading to the basement floors of her office building, I saw Hakone at the reception desk and caught her eye. While I was dithering about whether to go inside or not, Hakone said something in the ear of the other receptionist and came out to me, pushing open the glass door.

"San! What brings you here?" She was probably surprised by how much shopping I had.

"I was just passing by." I put down the stationer's branded bags. "Thank you so much for everything with the auction. It's quite a lot of work, isn't it, selling things online?"

Once I'd realized that taking photos for the listing was only the beginning of a process that involved a mountain of tasks like signing up for a seller ID and answering questions from watchers, I'd ended up passing the whole business over to the two of them.

When Hakone messaged me saying someone had asked when and where the refrigerator had been purchased, I took my time looking for the warranty. Then Senta called and said, "Sis, our rating goes down if we don't respond immediately." Apparently even a small drop in your rating meant that buyers would avoid doing business with you. I could hardly repay Hakone's kindness in letting us use her seller ID by damaging her reputation, so I'd looked frantically for the paperwork. The whole thing had been a weight on my mind until the buyer left feedback that they'd safely received the item.

"It's amazing that someone actually bought it for seventy thousand yen, though," Hakone said. "When we posted our old fridge, it got zero bids. Nothing."

"It is. Especially since I was planning to pay a waste collection company to get rid of it. Seventy thousand yen for that!"

"I'd never even heard of it, but I guess it's a really popular foreign brand?"

"I bet it was his ex-wife who'd wanted it to begin with. He'd never go for anything so flashy himself."

"But he sprang for it."

"He was trying to impress her. Oh, Hakone, I think you're being called." The other receptionist was waving and pointing to the phone.

"I'm almost done for the day, so if you want to wait a few minutes, I can leave with you."

"Okay. Why not, while I'm here?"

I followed Hakone into the waiting room. Inside the space, which smelled like disinfectant, a woman with long hair was sitting on the bench, head lowered, looking at the floor. "We get a lot of slightly strange patients here," Hakone had told me once, when I'd come in to get my teeth whitened.

"Strange?" I'd asked.

"Our clinic director doesn't believe in tooth extraction, and has books and gives talks about how you shouldn't let your dentist extract any teeth, no matter what. Because of that, we get patients from all over the country who believe their lives have been ruined by losing teeth under other doctors. Which gives it a different atmosphere from other clinics, I guess. I'd recommend going elsewhere for treatment."

Hakone was six years younger than I was, but it had been nearly ten years since Senta had first introduced us, so I didn't have to worry about her not feeling at ease to tell me what she really thought. She looked like a lady-in-waiting from a Doll Festival display, and I thought her creaseless eyelids were cute on her, but she seemed to have a complex about them and once seriously asked me whether I thought she should have plastic surgery. She had scaled my teeth for me when I'd come here before, even though, as far as I knew, she wasn't a qualified dental hygienist. Without thinking too deeply about it, I'd asked about some stubborn discoloration, whereupon she'd said, "I'm sure a quick polish will get rid of that for you," and had gone at the tooth surface with the drill. Thanks to that incident, I still had a tiny dimple on the bottom of one of my front teeth.

I sat on a bench behind the one where the other woman was, flipping through a magazine. Soon Hakone came out of the door behind the reception desk, having changed out of her uniform. When I got up, the bag with the construction paper rustled loudly, but the woman on the bench kept looking at the floor, as she'd done the whole time, and didn't move an inch.

"He says his ex-wife's been sending him strange garbled emails recently," I said. We'd found a table in the seating area of the department store's food hall. I was still thinking about the ex-wife following the refrigerator conversation.

"You must be concerned," said Hakone, sounding anything but as she took a pair of disposable chopsticks out of their packet.

"Maybe I should have gone for that one too," I said enviously, looking into Hakone's bento box as I took the rubber band off my own.

"You can have two slices of my steak if you give me some of your eel."

I'd brought her to the store, promising to buy her something new to wear, or anything else she wanted, but Hakone had headed straight for the escalator down to the basement food hall and asked for a bento. "I saw it on the local news the other day. They had a feature on department store deli eats, and the Spicy Fillet Steak Summer Set Bento just looked so delicious," she said, flattening her plump eyelids in anticipation.

Maybe partly because of the TV feature, the late-afternoon deli counters were thronged with people. Banners positioned around the floor advertised the Beat the Heat Bento Expo.

Hakone swiftly referred to the floor guide and said, "This way," and took off without sparing a glance at the stalls she passed. I followed, but never having been very good at walking through crowds, I kept barging into people's shoulders, and by the time I caught up, she had already joined the line for the steak bento. I'd planned to just wait for her, but I saw a banner for the Special Selection Four-Eel Taste Test Bento and was tempted into getting one. It featured eel sourced from the Shimanto River, Lake Hamana, the Mikawa region, and Miyazaki Prefecture, grilled both with sauce and without. I carefully took a piece of each and placed them on top of Hakone's rice.

"Do you think he's still getting them? The weird garbled messages?"

"Probably."

"Has he said?"

"No, but you can just tell these things sometimes."

"Huh. Aren't you worried? Didn't you say his ex-wife was really good-looking?"

"*Really* good-looking. Like that actress from the movies."

"And she's got long legs?"

"Really long legs."

"How did he split up with a person like that and end up marrying you?"

"I wonder." *What would you think if you saw his true form?* I thought. I shivered, then looked up and saw there was an AC vent embedded in the ceiling right above my head. "Hakone, are you and Senta thinking about getting married yet?" I asked, getting a light blouse out of my bag.

Hakone hummed and said nothing. She looked like she was giving it some serious thought. Her eyes were focused on the booth's cloud-glass partition, but her mouth was still chewing away steadily at the steak.

"Do you think he's too immature? Is that the problem?" I asked.

"No, it's not like that. I'm not sure why. Maybe I don't really know, myself. But I'd like us to stay as separate people for a little longer."

"Separate people?"

"I mean, getting married, that means swallowing everything about the other person, the good things and the bad. What if there ends up being more of the bad? You'd both be in trouble then, wouldn't you?" Hakone said. "Do you know the story of the snake ball? I don't remember where I read it. Maybe someone told it to me, a long time ago. There are two snakes, and they each start cannibalizing the other one's tail. And they eat and they eat at exactly the same speed, until they're just two heads making a ball, and then they both get eaten up and disappear. I think that's the image I have of marriage—that both me and the other person, as we are now, will disappear before we can do anything about it. But I guess that can't be right. I think?"

"Snake ball, huh?" I poked at a piece of grilled eel laid on the rice, and pictured a bright white ball covered in scales.

Hakone quenched her thirst with cold roasted green tea from the vending machine. "But it only applies when the snakes consume each other at the same rate. Between me and Senta, I might end up swallowing him all in one big gulp."

I took a mouthful of grilled eel seasoned with plenty of sansho pepper. The Lake Hamana eel was firmer and more succulent than the one from the Mikawa region.

I was secretly impressed by Hakone's story. Whenever I'd gotten close to someone in the past, I'd had the feeling that little by little I was being replaced. The other person's ideas, interests, and habits would gradually take the place of my own. Every time I noticed myself acting as though that was who I'd been all along, a chill went up my spine. The fact that I couldn't stop, even if I tried, was proof that it wasn't actually a matter of anything as benign as acting or pretending.

Men entered into me through my roots like nutrients dissolved in potting soil. Every time I got together with someone new, I got replanted, and the nutrients from the old soil disappeared without a trace. As if to prove it, I could hardly recall the men I'd been with before. Strangely, too, the men I'd been with had all wanted me to grow in them. Eventually, I'd start to feel in danger of root rot, and would hurriedly break the pot and uproot myself.

Was that the fault of the soil, or did the problem lie in the roots?

I'd expected marriage to be an even more constricting flower pot than my previous relationships. But after four years, I hadn't tried to escape from the soil that was my husband. Hearing Hakone's snake-ball story, I finally felt that something that had been cloudy to me had become clear. All this time, I had been feeding myself to those men. By now, I was like the ghost of a snake that had already been eaten up by many other snakes, and I'd lost my own body long before getting swallowed up by my husband. Didn't that explain why I didn't much mind whether it was a husband I was living with or something only resembling a husband?

One night, after dinner, I was surprised to notice my husband engrossed in his iPad rather than the variety show playing on the TV.

"What are you doing on there?" I peered over his shoulder.

"Huh?"

"Is it a game?"

"It's a game."

"What kind of game?"

There was no response. I gave up and cleared the table and went for a bath, but when I came back, my husband hadn't moved.

"Bath's free."

"Okay," I heard a muffled voice say. I finished towel-drying my hair and stepped out onto the balcony to bring in the laundry I'd hung out that afternoon. The zelkovas planted in a clump just beyond the railing were overgrown with green leaves that looked like a neglected hairdo. I recalled seeing a circular in the mailroom about plans to prune the plantings.

"Uwano recommended this game," my husband said at last.

I was folding laundry on the living room floor. "Uwano again? You're talking about him a lot lately."

"I think you should try it. It's good."

"No thanks. I don't like games."

"That's exactly what I told Uwano. Here, take it."

"I'm folding laundry."

"Let the cat do it. Go, Zoromi, go do it for her." He moved the cat off the space beside him where she'd been asleep, and beckoned to me. Normally he was never this insistent. I guessed he must be feeling needy.

My husband seemed anxious to make a snake ball with me. When he made me sit with him while he watched his variety shows, claiming it was more fun than watching alone, it had to be that he was trying to erase the chilly gaze that he felt I was directing at him. He probably thought that once he and I became one, he would never again have to worry about being judged by others.

I sat down on the couch and looked at the iPad screen. I was expecting some cutting-edge visual effects, but what I saw was an image representing what looked like oceans and continents, drawn in simple lines like in old Nintendo games. Small discs of different colors twinkled all across the map.

"What are these?" I asked.

"Oh, those," my husband said, turning his shoulders toward me. "Coins."

"And what do I do with these coins?"

"Touch one and see," he said, so I tried pressing on a brown disc with my finger. I heard a tinkling sound like coins dropping into a piggy bank, which I'd been hearing constantly all evening. I waited for something else to happen, but that was it.

"It didn't do anything."

"Look at the bottom of the screen. You've banked some money."

Sure enough, there was a number at the lower-right-hand corner of the screen. "This is a game where you collect money?"

"Yeah." My husband nodded while sucking on a strip of dried squid.

"Are there any bad guys?"

"Huh? Bad guys? No."

"So you collect the money, and then what?"

"When you've collected enough, you can buy your own land."

"You buy your own land, and then? What happens then?"

"More land gives you more coins."

"Does it?"

"Yeah. Then you collect those, so you can bank money again. Then you can buy even more land."

I didn't say what I was thinking, but he must have sensed it.

He pulled the strip of squid from his mouth, and said, "It's because you're a housewife, San. You can't understand how men don't want to have to think about things when we get home."

"What is it you want to avoid thinking about that badly?"

"The answers to questions like that, for example. Hey, give it back if you're not even going to play." My husband took the iPad from my hand and sank his head back to the game. I fled from the tinkling of coins falling and the suckling sound of him chewing on dried squid.

After that, my husband took to tinkling the fake coins incessantly, everywhere—in the bath, on the toilet, even under the covers. "Why don't you try a different game?" I'd ask, but he'd only say, "I like this one."

I could have understood if the game offered a vision of a wonderful world more exciting than real life. But what was so appealing about the insipid map that looked like a stage backdrop and its ever-twinkling coins? I thought perhaps the game got more interesting the longer you played, but whenever I looked over my husband's shoulder, the screen always looked the same. It seemed that all he was doing was almost robotically placing his finger on the discs. Every time I would ask, "You really enjoy it that much?" he'd say, "That's not what it's about," in a curiously languid tone.

"Hey, do we have any more of those pears someone gave us the other day? The pears?"

My husband looked up from the iPad for the first time in a while, and what I saw nearly made me shriek and run from the room. The positioning of his features was deteriorating faster than ever. His face was barely maintaining a form that could even be recognized as human.

He seemed not to realize that anything was amiss, and simply looked at me with his terrifyingly wide-set eyes, and said, "Are they all gone?"

"No," I said. I was feigning calm, but my voice came out higher than normal.

"Can you peel me one?"

"Okay." I turned on my heel and went back into the kitchen. There was a tremor in my hand holding the paring knife.

When I served him the peeled pear segments on a plate, the husband-like creature excitedly reached for a cocktail stick. "You know, I think pears might be my favorite fruit," he announced.

How could he even see straight? The husband-like thing

picked up the cocktail stick and popped a pear segment into the mouth, which was positioned perilously close to his jawline. His teeth must have been in their right place, because they made a champing sound as he chewed.

"Aren't you going to have any?" the husband-like thing said.

I wasn't sure that I wanted to. But it would have been suspicious for me to say no.

When I sat down next to him, the husband-like thing picked up the TV remote and started flipping through channels.

"This really takes me back." On the screen, a quiz show was posing a question about an ad that had been on heavy rotation just after we'd gotten married. "We used to sing this song all the time. Remember?"

Instead of responding, I looked down and nibbled a slice of pear.

"Do you remember, on our honeymoon, how I chewed up all the fruit for you so you could eat it?"

"You did?" I said distractedly.

"Sure. You'd just gotten braces, and you said the metal hurt and you couldn't eat anything. So I ordered a fruit platter from room service, and chewed it all up and spat it out onto the plate, and gave it to you."

"You fed me fruit you'd already eaten?"

"And you smiled and ate it all." The husband-like thing's voice sounded indistinct, as if it were coming from behind a wall of water. "Maybe that's why it's so easy being with you.

When you did that, I knew you'd probably eat up my poop with a smile too."

That night, my husband left the iPad outside the bedroom. For the first time in months, his hand crept into my bed, under my comforter. I wanted to pretend I was asleep, but then he went to switch on the light, so I reached out and caught his hand almost by reflex.

In the darkness, my husband swiftly removed my pajama bottoms. When I thought about whether the thing that had started to move on top of me was my husband or just something like him, I felt a terrible dread and kept my eyes firmly shut. Then I felt skin slacken, and bodies start to yield, and then I could no longer tell whose sensations I was feeling. *Snake ball!* My body was starting to coil, and I tried to stop thinking by closing my eyes even more tightly. That only made the boundary between the skin of our entwined bodies even hazier. My husband the snake opened his mouth and swallowed me headfirst, and I desperately resisted his sticky, moist membranes, but soon the inside of his body became a pleasurable place to be. By then I was actively feeding my body to him to be devoured. He seemed to be enjoying eating me up so much that the sensation of it spread to me, and I felt as though I were tasting my own self.

•

After Hasebo's wedding had come and gone, and I'd returned to my usual sequence of undistinguished days, I ran into Kitae by the checkout in the pharmacy.

"My," Kitae said, her voice clear and effortless, "it's been quite a while since I saw you. How have you been?"

"Fine, thank you." For some reason I couldn't meet her eyes. I bowed and looked down at the floor where it reflected the fluorescent lights.

Kitae, who'd joined the line after me, looked into my basket and pointed. "I use the same fabric conditioner. Isn't it good?" and then strode off over to the kitchen goods aisle.

I decided to wait for her outside the pharmacy. The cicadas were chirring at full volume. As I was comparing prices on brands of toilet paper, Kitae came out of the automatic sliding doors carrying full bags. "San, dear, you're looking a little tan," she said, studying me closely from head to toe.

"Am I?"

"You certainly are. You used to be all pasty, like a sheet of paper."

"I've been busy with errands lately," I said, instinctively stepping backward under the shade of the awning.

"That must be why I haven't seen you around." I couldn't decide whether she'd believed me or whether she'd just accepted my excuse.

"And have you been well?" I hesitated about asking after Sansho, leaving an awkward pause in the conversation.

Kitae seemed preoccupied by the tatami shop opposite the pharmacy, saying something about the owner. "His wife's sick, poor man. They're going through a hard time." She started walking slowly up the slight hill of the main street.

I hurriedly fell into step.

"Where do you normally shop?" Kitae asked, a little out of breath.

"Where do I shop?" Similarly out of breath, I looked up toward the new supermarket that stood at the top of the hill. I used it often, because it had a wide selection and good prices.

"Oh, that place. I thought so," Kitae said, sounding disappointed.

"Is it bad?"

"I wouldn't say bad," she said. "It's just that as soon as it opened, everyone started shopping there. Isn't it such a shame when we have such a traditional Japanese main street right here?" She waved to the employee sitting behind the counter in the dry cleaner's. "Of course, I understand the appeal of being able to pay for everything at once, but you lose the human touch, don't you." At the middle of the hill, she stopped to catch her breath. She watched the line of people waiting to buy a bento outside the Chinese restaurant, then took out her usual white terrycloth handkerchief and wiped her brow. "So, San, are you about to do your shopping now?"

I nodded. I'd been thinking about tonight's menu as I left the apartment.

"Then come with me for a bit."

"You mean to the local shops?" I asked.

"I'll introduce you to my grocer, and the butcher, and the fishmonger I use." She neatly folded away her handkerchief, and set off purposefully, overtaking a young person wheeling a bicycle.

"And so the mountains ended up being the best solution."

I couldn't tell if Senta was listening or not, because he was stuffing his mouth with prosciutto while making small huffing noises. He seemed to be in a rush to get his next plate of food, even though I'd told him there were no time restrictions. Hakone, who'd taken a spoonful each of several different dishes on an appetizer plate, sat down beside Senta and started intently conveying food to her mouth.

"It's so different from our usual all-you-can-eat place," she said, cradling her cheeks in her palms as she savored the mixed seafood marinée. "The place Senta and I always go has so many choices, it's almost a joke. We assumed that was the point of going all-you-can-eat, but actually, the better places stick to what they're good at, I guess. Or it's more like they really refine each dish."

A server stopped by the side of our table, so I asked for a refill of sparkling water.

"We're in your debt. You took me out once already, and now you're treating us to this high-class all-you-can-eat," Hakone said.

"It's called a buffet," Senta butted in.

"Don't worry about it. A thousand-yen bento to thank you for seventy thousand yen? And I knew Senta would enjoy it too."

Hakone picked up the finely decorated bowl of chilled vegetable potage.

"We've been going hungry since last night to make the most of it, Sis."

"No problem," I said vaguely, and sipped my freshly poured sparkling water. I'd invited them to a hotel lunch because I'd recalled Senta grousing about not being allowed to eat his fill when they ate out.

While I received an agreed-upon amount each month from my husband for living expenses, Senta and Hakone shared their finances, even though they weren't married yet. Hakone held the purse strings and, having a good head for money, made a rule of feeding Senta a bowl of rice before they went out to eat. Since Hakone was the one bringing in most of the income right now, Senta couldn't really complain.

"So does either of you know a good mountain somewhere?" I ladled a spoonful of curry from a silver sauce boat over my saffron rice. I'd deliberated for a while between it and the beef stroganoff, but in the end I'd given in to the curry's dark allure.

"A mountain? Do you mean for the camper van trip?"

"This is a different mountain."

"She's going to abandon a cat," Senta said.

"What? No! You're throwing Zoromi out?" Hakone said, looking up from her platter.

"No, no. Not Zoromi. It's a cat belonging to someone I know."

"Oh. I thought you meant Zoromi!"

"I'm not going to abandon Zoromi. This person's cat started peeing all over the apartment. It's been a year, and they've tried everything. She and her husband finally decided to let him go live in the mountains." I spooned more curry onto my rice.

" 'Go live' is one way of putting it," Senta added quietly. "Sis, aren't you gonna tell them the truth?"

"I don't need to—she knows, really." That was why Kitae had held on to Sansho all summer. "She promised her husband she'd do it once the weather gets a little cooler." After taking me shopping at the local shops, Kitae had bowed her head and asked whether I could drive them up to a mountain somewhere. I sighed. "I hate a problem without a good solution."

Maybe this was the kind of thing my husband was trying to avoid too, by playing his game all the time.

"I'm going for the grilled duck breast." Senta stood up.

Hakone, busy coiling spaghetti carbonara and spaghetti pescatore alternately onto her fork, didn't even glance his way.

"Is Senta always like that? Even at home?" I asked. I tried to recall what he'd been like growing up.

"Like that? Yeah, I guess he is," Hakone said, head tilted, seeming not to understand the question.

Just as I thought—his face doesn't degenerate like my husband's.
I said, "I guess he's not a man with many worries."

"No." Hakone nodded thoughtfully. "But his screenplays always seem to be full of really conflicted characters. Which makes me laugh. Because when he's at home he's usually got a belly full of cabbage, you know? I mean, I pad his meals out with cabbage just to make the other dishes go further. So I always think, why doesn't he make a film about cabbage? I think that'd be a lot more interesting. Don't you?"

I looked toward Senta as he prowled back and forth in front of the silver trays of food. "Maybe you're right. That could be interesting."

Senta went back to the buffet for two more helpings after that. "The beef stroganoff and curry on rice combo works better than you'd think," he said as he shoveled it into his mouth.

Hakone got a small mountain of cake from the dessert section, and expressed regret at having to leave more than half of it.

I paid and met the two of them at the hotel entrance where they'd been waiting. They bowed at me like flunkies, saying, "Thank you for the meal," in unison.

As I was waving goodbye and walking away, Senta came running back toward me. "Sis! The mountains you were asking about earlier? How about Gunma Prefecture?"

"Gunma?"

"I just remembered that when I went out there to help a

friend's shoot, there were some mountains there that looked pretty untouched. There might be animals living there."

"I didn't know that."

"I'll send you the address later."

"Yes, please."

Senta turned on his heel again and ran off into the station.

After taking a stroll around town and doing some shopping, I came home to find my husband's work shoes in the entryway.

It was only 4:00 p.m. Wondering whether he was back from work already, I called out, "I'm home!" There was no answer.

I left my shopping in the hallway and went into the living room. On the table was an empty glass and an open container of the sweet-and-savory sautéed shishito peppers I'd made ahead and stashed in the refrigerator. I picked them both up and moved them to the sink in the kitchen along with a pair of abandoned chopsticks, and went back out into the hallway, saying, "Anybody home?" This time, I encountered a pair of suit trousers and a dress shirt on the floor, still retaining a somewhat human form.

I picked up the clothes and knocked on the door to my husband's room. When I opened it, Zoromi, who had been curled up on top of my husband's desk, looked at me, got up, and thrust his front legs forward in a stretch. He must have gotten trapped inside. He made an affectionate sound and brushed up against my shin.

I hung up the suit jacket on a clothes hanger and moved toward the bedroom with Zoromi.

My husband was sitting with his back against the headboard, dressed in T-shirt and sweatpants, playing on the iPad again. Even though it was daytime, he had the curtains shut tight.

"What happened to work?" I was secretly exasperated. *If he was here, why hadn't he answered me?*

"I've been feeling kind of sluggish." My husband didn't look up from the game. His voice was so faint, it was nearly drowned out by the tinkling sound of the coins.

"You should see a doctor." I picked up a pair of socks from the floor beside the bed. As soon as I said it, though, I found myself doubting whether it was really the kind of problem a doctor could help with.

"San, what would you do if I died?"

I'd moved toward the window to draw the curtains, but I stopped and turned around. "What are you talking about?"

"Uwano told me something his wife said recently, when it turned out her dog needed surgery. She said that if the dog died, she'd be more upset than if he died."

I pictured Uwano's rosy, macaque-like face. That must have been a blow.

"I feel like you'd be pretty indifferent too, considering," my husband said.

Without replying, I flung the curtains open. Sunlight leapt

into the room through the glass. My husband looked up at me for a moment, but the shafts of light and the dust rising from the bedclothes prevented me from seeing his face clearly.

"Could be a summer slump," he said, eyes back on the screen.

"Could be a summer slump," I said.

"Something good to eat might do the trick," he said.

"Something good to eat might do the trick," I repeated, and left the bedroom, which was suffused by my husband's smell.

But his condition didn't improve. His color looked worse and worse every day. He was managing to go to work but didn't seem to be sleeping well. Even his once-formidable appetite dropped off, and he lost weight. He went to a doctor but was only told, non-committally, that it could be a case of late-summer slump.

I tried to get my husband to quit playing the game. But he said that would only make him feel worse, and he continued to collect the tinkling coins as if he'd been possessed.

"It's a mantra," Kitae said, pulling the tab on a canned coffee.

"A mantra? The game?" I said, shuffling my butt around on the bench, which was damp from the previous day's rain.

"Yes. I think your husband's trying to shut all his troubles and worries and anxieties out of his mind. Which is why he needs to *tap-tap-tap* all the time."

"You mean like in the story of Hoichi the Earless," I said.

"I hadn't even thought of that, but maybe. Of course, there's also the possibility he's desperately hiding from some kind of temptation."

"Temptation?" I was surprised.

"Yes, temptation. You haven't noticed anything?"

The only possibility that the word "temptation" brought to mind was the issue of his ex-wife. My husband hadn't mentioned her since that one conversation, and I'd assumed the whole thing had blown over. But what had actually happened?

Kitae looked at the dogs playing and chasing each other around. "I'd be doing everything I could for you, if I weren't so distracted myself," she said, and sighed. "You're going through such a difficult time too—I'm so sorry," apologizing for the fourth time that day.

We were setting a date to abandon Sansho.

Kitae had been postponing it every Sunday, saying, "We'll wait until it's just a little cooler," but the situation had finally come to a head. Their whole apartment smelled foul, and a neighbor had raised a complaint.

Kitae had grown haggard. "So, Gunma Prefecture," she said, as though she were trying to work up some enthusiasm for the idea.

"Yes. I haven't been there myself either, but as far as I can tell online, it looks like there are several species of animals living there too."

"Do you suppose there are bears?"

"It is a mountain, after all."

"Yes," Kitae said, and sighed deeply again. "I'm so sorry. You must excuse me. When you've gone to so much trouble."

Maybe because the evening was slightly cooler, there were more dogs in the dog run than usual. Kitae wasn't saying anything more, so I watched the dogs and drank the coffee, which had gone warm.

I was listening to the voices of children laughing when Kitae said, "I've been thinking about how little it takes to bring happiness crumbling down. I couldn't have imagined any of this would happen when I decided to get Sansho. To have a husband and a cat to live with, that was everything I wanted. I thought I was all set. Who would have thought the cat pee—! It just makes you think," she said. "Cat pee, of all things!"

A dog barked, and one of the dog owners who had been chatting nearby pointed to what the dog was looking at, and said, "Dragonfly! Dragonfly!"

"Maybe I ought to try to disappear into a game, myself," Kitae said. The way she said it, I couldn't quite take it as a joke.

I left the apartment complex to shop for dinner. Ever since Kitae's recommendation, I'd switched over to shopping at the local shops on the main street. Prices were higher than at the supermarket, and it was more trouble paying separately at each shop, but even so, I felt like taking time and trouble over something added dimension to my bland life.

The way I was living now was like being exiled on an island. The isolated island was certainly a kind of paradise, with abundant fruit trees and animals I could frolic with to my heart's content, but even so, I'd occasionally be overcome with longing for where I used to be. When I was newly married, I felt that the island would ruin me if I stayed on it, and I often seriously considered escape. But then I'd quickly remember about having to fight for fruit or endure the petty discomforts of living with others, and I remained a drifting resident of this utopia, cut off from everyone else.

When I turned the corner of the flower shop, a brightly colored rose moss caught my eye. Now that it was September, the plants and flowers on display were starting to have an autumnal feel. The word Kitae had used earlier—"temptation"—resurfaced in my mind. Picking out tomatoes at the grocery store, I tried to conjure up an image of my husband's ex-wife, whom I'd only seen in photographs, to picture her propositioning him, but before it could happen, my husband's face started to collapse. The whole scene seemed so completely unlikely.

The prospect of one day finding myself more upset by losing a pet than a husband—like Uwano's wife—hit much closer to home than the worry that my husband would get back together with his ex.

As I hunted through a cardboard box for the shapeliest daikon, a boy of grade-school age slipped past me and said, "Here you are, mister," and handed a scrap of paper and a one-thousand-yen note to the shopkeeper.

"That's today's, then. Well done, lad. See you again tomorrow."

The boy took the bag of vegetables and the change, and left the shop with a sullen expression on his face.

Now that was a shopping technique I hadn't considered, I thought admiringly, but then I accidentally made eye contact with the shopkeeper, and feeling awkward, I said, "I'd like some bran pickle, please. One eggplant."

Maybe what was tempting my husband wasn't the ex-wife, but a voice that said, *There's no need to live life just keeping up the appearance of being human.* The thought came into my head as I looked down at the shopkeeper's baseball cap as he crouched to get my pickles. "I'll throw in the turnip tail for free," the shopkeeper said, and stood up holding the bag of pickles, bringing the sharp, sour smell of fermented rice bran to my nostrils.

When I got home, my husband was in the kitchen deep-frying something.

The whole time we were dating, and since we'd been married, he'd never once cooked anything.

"What's going on?" I asked, shocked.

"I saw it on TV and just felt like trying it out," he said, without even looking up. He'd been in bed a lot recently—was he feeling better?

"I'm impressed you figured it out," I said. When I looked

around the stove where he was standing, I saw a jumble of brand-new cooking equipment, including a thermometer and some metal trays for laying out the hot food to soak up excess oil. "I didn't know where to find everything, so I bought what I needed from the supermarket," he said.

"What about work?"

"I left early."

"Okay." I started putting my groceries away into the refrigerator and the pantry. What had happened to the mantra, the temptation? The question was in my throat, but the sound of the oil popping and the whine of the extractor fan surrounded my husband like a wall, and there was no opening for me to speak to him.

"Sit down, San. I'm making us the deep-fried special tonight," he said in a slightly injured tone. Apparently, I was getting in his way.

I took a seat on the couch, where my husband usually sat. Zoromi had followed me, so I stroked her fur for a while, but I still felt unsettled. "Do you need me to show you where the paper towels are? You can use the grill rack that came with the microwave to let the oil drip off." As I commented on this and that, my husband brought me a highball and plonked it down on the table.

"You sit and drink this and watch some TV," he said, and picked up the remote and pressed play on a variety show he'd recorded. Without another word, I did what he said, and sat and sipped at the highball, which was a drink I didn't even like. I tried concentrating on the TV screen, but the show's appeal was entirely beyond me.

After a half hour or so, I heard him say, "Here it comes," and when I went to the table I saw a mound of fritters on a large serving platter, the bran pickles I'd bought earlier, inexpertly sliced, and two empty glasses laid out in a plausible way. There were even small dishes for condiments, with a choice of salt, sauce, or lemon juice.

"Quick, San," my husband said, and I sat in my seat and picked up my chopsticks.

My husband sat down next to me, took the top off a bottle of beer, and started pouring it into my empty glass.

"What's going on?" I said again. I couldn't help feeling spooked.

"It makes a nice change, doesn't it?" My husband poured himself a beer as well, held it up, and said, "Cheers." His Adam's apple moved happily up and down. He drank so fast it was as if the beer were soaking straight into his body.

I had a mouthful as well. The mild bitterness and alcohol content spread through my mouth and felt pleasant.

"They're best eaten hot."

I tentatively extended my chopsticks toward the fritters piled on the serving dish. They looked a little lumpy, but the batter was a tawny golden color. My appetite whetted by the smell and the sound that had pervaded the room, I dabbed salt on the batter and threw it in my mouth.

It was good. I'd feared that it might be undercooked, but the filling was the ideal texture, and the batter made a satisfying crispy sound between my teeth.

"Where did you learn to do this?" I said, huffing as I moved the hot fritter loosely around my mouth.

"It's my first time," he said, huffing like me.

"It looks like you got your appetite back."

For the first time in a good while, he seemed to be enjoying his food. He reached for another fritter and said, "Yeah." There was much more I wanted to ask, but he just kept saying, "Best hot, San," so I dutifully shoveled down the fritters. Onion rings. Squid. Prawn. Sweet potato. Chicken. They were all tasty. I had them with sauce, and then with lemon juice, and the mountain on the serving dish, which I'd thought we could hardly finish between the two of us, began diminishing before our eyes. In silence we devoured the fritters and guzzled down more beer. I couldn't remember the last time I'd had this much to drink.

"So you're feeling better," I said, slightly drunkenly, once my belly was filled up. I could feel a rosy flush around my eyes.

My husband was still eating in silence, picking up the fritters with his fingers now rather than his chopsticks.

"What do you think it was, in the end? I know it wasn't the summer slump," I said. My husband cocked his head to one side as if to say, *Yeah, I don't know what it was*, and I heard myself laugh. I felt relaxed for the first time in months. "By the way, I was telling Miss Kitae about the game today, and she asked whether you're feeling tempted by something."

"Something?"

"She didn't say what. But I guess there was no need to worry," I said, and laughed again, louder.

Then I noticed there wasn't even a smile on my husband's face, and my expression sobered.

"You *are* feeling better, aren't you?" I asked again.

My husband didn't respond, and continued eating, keeping his reptilian eyes cast down at his plate.

I looked at his expressionless profile and remembered that I hadn't seen his face from the front in a long time.

I took a long swig of my beer.

"Maybe I'll go into business, open a fritter joint," my husband said quietly, licking the oil off his fingers. His voice sounded both like my husband's and like that of a complete stranger, and though the last mouthful of beer suddenly tasted of nothing, I gulped it down without meaning to.

I went to see Hasebo in her and her husband's new place, and got home late afternoon to find my husband, who seemed to have left work early again, standing pensively in front of a pan of oil, holding a pair of cooking chopsticks.

"Should we open a window?"

The heat of the frying had steamed up the apartment. My husband, who'd been gazing into the pan as if he were searching for his long-lost mother, finally reacted to the beep emitted by the

AC remote and said, "San, welcome home." It sounded hollow, as if half of him was still wandering through some dream.

The tray on the countertop held a lavish pile of battered and breaded ingredients. *Not again.* Just the sight of it seemed to bring last night's fritters back up to my throat. Truthfully, my stomach had begged for mercy long ago. But what was the right thing to do when a sick person told you the only thing that gave him relief was deep-frying fritters?

It turned out that the fritters were just a replacement for the coin-tinkling game, and my husband was still unwell.

He once again installed me on the couch and handed me a highball. Helpless to refuse this strangely solicitous husband, I brought the glass to my lips and stared dimly at the variety show. There was still nothing interesting to me about it. But soon enough, between the sounds of deep-frying coming from the kitchen and the cacophonous cries on the TV, I felt a mist descend over my head. Stirring from the couch seemed like a huge effort.

"Tell me where you've been today," my husband said, having moved me to the table and eagerly poured me a beer.

He sounded almost like a wife, I thought. "To Hasebo's new place."

Beside me, I thought I saw my husband nod. But maybe he didn't nod—maybe he was just staring at me. I felt an uneasy rustling down the left side of my body as I picked up my chopsticks. I moistened my mouth with the pleasantly foamy beer and picked up a fritter as I was told. No rice, no miso soup—my husband was only interested in deep frying. "That's bamboo shoot. And that one, that's chum with yam bulbs," he told me proudly. "I've made a light ponzu sauce for you tonight." My husband said his digestion wasn't so good lately, and he hardly touched the platter, making me eat most of it.

I put the fritter in my mouth resignedly. But to my surprise, the moment I tasted the first piece, my appetite came back with a vengeance, and I found myself reaching for the next fritter even before I'd swallowed the first. Perhaps my body was starting to need the oil. I tossed one fritter after another into my mouth. Washed down with beer, they made me feel warm and excited inside. I'd keep eating them forever if I could. I got so absorbed in moving my mouth I couldn't think about anything else.

"It's nice you're getting to be more like me," I heard my husband murmur as he poured himself another beer.

What? I thought, but my mouth was full of fritter and I couldn't respond.

I hurriedly tried to swallow, but he said, "Try this on the next one," and pressed the yuzu-chili paste on me, and as I chewed the next fritter, I found that I couldn't for the life of me recall what he'd said or what I'd wanted to say in reply.

Belly full, I let myself be led by the hand to the couch, and gazed at the variety show with him. "It's so easy being with you," my husband said, as though intoning some kind of spell, so I replied, "You're right." I hadn't even stopped to think about what I was saying.

•

When I woke up and looked in the mirror, I saw that my face had finally begun to forget who I was.

I guessed my features had just been caught off guard that day. When I peered closer, they rushed to reassemble, as though to say, *Oh, shit*. But it was as if they couldn't remember their original placement, and as a result, the final impression was a little off-kilter.

I took another, harder look in the mirror. The eyes were a little too far apart, making the whole face look curiously stretched out.

I was becoming like my husband.

Trying to pull myself together, I washed my face, sluicing it repeatedly with water. Then I used my fingers to smooth on a stronger sunscreen than I normally used. There was a voice in my head that said, *What's the point of going to all this effort over a face that was neither here nor there to begin with?* But I managed to ignore it, and left the apartment just on time.

When I took the car out and drove it up the ramp from the complex's underground car park, Kitae and her husband were waiting by the exit at the top, as we'd arranged.

I got out of the driver's seat and said, "Thanks for meeting me," and bowed to them. *"Thanks" isn't really the right word*, I thought as the words left my mouth, but I didn't know what else to say.

Kitae's husband seemed to be in the same boat. "No, thank

you," he said, and bowed much more politely than I had. Next to him, Kitae was cradling the soft pet carrier hanging from her shoulder as if it were her child.

Seen close up, her husband was smaller than I'd imagined. As with Kitae, all the color seemed to have fallen neatly out of his hair. And because he was dressed in pale shades, he again reminded me of a statue of the jizo standing on the side of some country road.

"San, dear, this is my husband, Arai." She turned to her husband. "Arai, this is my friend San," she said, almost carelessly. "San's had cats for a long time, since she was small. She understands them much better than we do. So we can leave it up to her, Arai, and everything will be fine."

Kitae then turned to the mesh panel in the pet carrier, and leaned down to it. "Sansho, you don't need to be scared either. San's going to find a wonderful mountain for you."

I was a little daunted by the weight of the responsibility that seemed to have been placed on me, but I got the two of them into the back seat and said, "Okay, here we go," and loaded the GPS with the address of the Young People's Nature Camp in Gunma Prefecture that Senta had sent me. The estimated travel time was two and a half hours.

"It's nearer than I thought," said Kitae. She leaned forward and looked closely at the GPS screen. "That means we can go visit anytime, if worse comes to worst."

Could they? It would take five hours to get there and back. I thought Mr. Arai might be more realistic about this, but he didn't say anything, so I acted as if I hadn't heard anything either. Just as we set off, Sansho gave a small cry inside the carrier, but I also pretended not to have heard that.

Once we'd been on the Joshinetsu Expressway for a while, the mountain range came into view. Because it was a clear day, with what seemed like an impossibly high autumn sky, the profiles of the mountains stood out clearly, seeming to advance on us. The view was so impressive that I would have applauded, if not for the situation.

We exited onto local roads and advanced toward the mountains, following the GPS. The houses, which had been clustered together, soon began to be spaced out, then became sporadic, and finally disappeared. As we climbed up an endless series of switchbacks, we found ourselves deep enough in the woods that I braced myself for animals leaping out onto the road at any moment. According to the GPS, the Young People's Nature Camp was still farther ahead, but I found a gravel track and decided to follow it.

Soon after getting in the car, Kitae had said she was going to open the pet carrier. She must have been holding Sansho on her lap the whole way.

"Look! We're in the mountains. What do you think?" Kitae was talking to Sansho. When the gravel track petered out into a narrow dirt path, I stopped the car. It didn't seem to be a recognized road—the GPS screen showed a red arrow that indicated we should turn back.

No one spoke until I said, "We're here."

I was wondering whether or not to switch off the engine when Mr. Arai said to Kitae, almost in a whisper, "Hear that? We're here."

"Uh-huh." Kitae nodded but stayed in the back seat holding Sansho, head lowered.

"Is it different from what you expected?" I twisted my body around to face Mr. Arai.

He made a small smile, angling the corners of his eyes down, and shook his head. "Come on, Kitae," he said. "You decided. You can't change your mind now that we've come all this way."

Kitae said, "Yes, yes," but didn't raise her head.

I said, "I'm going to have a look around," and got out of the car. The second I opened the door, my body was enveloped by the natural chill of the mountain, and I found myself breathing in as deeply as I could. The air was humid and seemed to snuggle up against my skin. I retied the laces on my sneakers and walked ahead on the path.

I could hear sounds of birds everywhere. Were they singing from the tops of the trees? No matter how hard I tried to train my ears on their voices, I couldn't tell what direction they were coming from. I'd expected the mountains in fall to be cool, but because the sunlight was blocked by the trees, it was so cold that

I was almost shivering. Between the tall trees and bushes, I could see clumps of scabrous gentian and hairless salvia. Perhaps there'd been dew on the leaves—I noticed my socks were wet, and turned back toward the parked car.

It seemed that Mr. Arai was desperately trying to soothe Kitae. I couldn't tell exactly from a distance, but I could see Kitae, still holding Sansho and refusing to look up, and Mr. Arai's head moving as he was talking to her.

I was hoping that one of us would say, *Let's go back home after all.* There was no way Sansho was going to survive here. He'd have had more of a chance at the local shrine. But Kitae had said, "If he's near people, he'll get hit by a car." As a child, she had witnessed a neighbor's cat try to cross the road and get flattened.

I realized that by indulging Kitae's ideas about "the mountains," I'd started to subscribe to the idea that once we got here, Sansho would thrive. But it was clearly impossible. *My husband is the one we should be returning to the mountains*, I thought, remembering him at Machu Picchu, and how he'd moved about there as though he'd been brought back to life.

I picked my way carefully through the trees back to the car, and found Kitae sitting on a nearby stump with the pet carrier on her knees.

"How's Sansho doing?" I asked, thinking to myself, *Oh no, Mr. Arai's managed to convince her.*

"Sansho—well, he seems to be quite calm about it all," Kitae said, and pulled on the carrier's zipper and peeled back the nylon flap that covered the top.

"Sansho," she called, and Sansho raised his head, sniffing. "See? We're in the mountains now. Your new home. You can pee anywhere you want. Everywhere! You're going to be happy here."

Sansho swiveled his ears and peered around cautiously, but after a while he stood up inside the bag and thrust the top half of his body out of the opening.

He's getting away, I thought, and almost as soon as I did, Kitae grabbed his head and pushed him back down inside the carrier.

"No, no, no," she said, looking like she might cry, and shook her head petulantly.

Why don't we just head home? The words were in my mouth, but I managed to hold them back. They'd be easy to say. But then what?

Mr. Arai came back from his reconnaissance of the area and looked at Kitae stooped over on the stump, and me standing like a log beside her. He seemed to comprehend everything.

"Kitae, let me take care of it. I'll go leave him over there," he said calmly, as if he were telling her he'd lend a hand with the dishes.

"Arai. Did you say 'leave' him?" Kitae snapped, but in a voice so weak I wouldn't have imagined it belonged to her. The words seemed to take the last of her resolve, and after that she would only say, "Oh, no. Oh, no. Ah. Oh, no."

Mr. Arai gently lifted the carrier from Kitae's lap, and turned to me. "I'll just be a minute, then."

"Right, okay," I said, and then added, "I'll come with you."

Mr. Arai lowered his brows for a moment, looking concerned, and then glanced toward the back of Kitae's head.

"It's fine. Go. That's why we asked her to come," she said, still looking down, and Mr. Arai nodded and started to walk off.

When we were a little distance away, I thought I heard Kitae's voice from behind us, saying, "Oh, ah," but it sounded uncertain, and I didn't know whether she was angry or relieved.

The slender Mr. Arai strode up the mountain path ahead of me. Sansho, in the carrier hanging from his shoulder, must have weighed twelve pounds at least, but Mr. Arai followed the trail confidently, as though it were a walking route in a city park.

I was frantically following, carrying the backpack Kitae had loaded into the trunk of the car. Thanks to the extra weight, I gulped at the air like a fish poking its face out of water.

With each step, the soles of my sneakers sank into the soft ground. The deeper we went up the mountain, the more oxygenated the air seemed. I could feel the breathing of the trees, the soil, and the things that were turning back into soil.

While I was distracted by the sound of insects, Mr. Arai, ahead of me, suddenly turned his face to one side like a wild animal. He seemed to have sensed something, and started climbing straight up the slope, easing through narrow gaps between trees.

I followed with difficulty to a large rocky area where the ground leveled out. Water was flowing from one end.

"A rock spring," I said, out of breath. "How did you know?"

"I grew up surrounded by mountains," Mr. Arai said in a voice as clear as a bell, and carefully took the carrier off his shoulder and put it on the ground. "What do you think of this place?"

It seemed safer than the surrounding area, with better visibility and good hiding places under the rocks, but also more dangerous, considering the possibility of other animals.

"Seems good, I think," I said haltingly. Nowhere was truly safe.

Mr. Arai nodded briefly. "We'll do it here." And maybe out of kindness for how much I was sweating, he said, "Shall we sit down? There's a good view."

Kitae's backpack held a surprising number of items: dry cat food, canned food, plates, Sansho's favorite blanket, toys, bottled water, a collapsible cat house made of nylon.

"The other animals will notice Sansho straightaway if we leave these out," Mr. Arai said, sitting down on a convenient rock, voicing exactly the thought that was in my head. "What was Kitae thinking of, a picnic?"

"How long have you and she been married?" I asked, changing the subject even though I thought it might sound rude, so I wouldn't have to think about Sansho inside the bag.

"Married? Let's see, I think we're coming up to forty-five years."

"You got married young."

"I was twenty-five and Kitae was twenty-two, or thereabouts. I thought we could have waited a little longer, but you know how Kitae won't budge once she's set her mind to something."

"The two of you aren't at all alike," I said, and Mr. Arai seemed amused. Even though he didn't laugh, I could see it in the depths of his eyes. *He'd be a hard man to keep secrets from*, something inside me said.

"You know, I've seen you and your husband together before," he said.

"Really?"

"Yes. But you seemed a little different then, I think."

"I've gained fifteen pounds," I confessed, embarrassed, but Mr. Arai looked at me steadily, and quietly said, "Yes. That might be part of it, but I think you were also looking more . . . humanlike."

Humanlike. "I don't look human now?" I said, laughing to cover up my shock at his startling words.

"I'm sorry. That's a funny thing to say when we've only just met. Please—it was just something that came to mind—don't worry about it."

"No, it's actually . . . It's something I've noticed myself."

"It is?" Mr. Arai gazed at me again. I looked down at where the water welled up from the rock as though I were trying to pass unnoticed by some wild animal.

"Kitae's told you about the couple who became identical? The wife had come to me for advice, and in fact I was the one who suggested putting down a stone. It might be best if you were to place something between you and your husband too. Shall we?" Mr. Arai got up.

Looking at his white shirt, which was still pristine even after walking so far, I stood hurriedly to follow him.

As soon as she saw us coming back, Kitae jumped out of the car.

"Arai! You must have gone a long way. Did you set Sansho free somewhere nice? He won't be attacked by a bear, will he?" The skin around her eyes was puffy and red.

"It's all right. We found a good spot for him," Mr. Arai said slowly, and patted her shoulder as though brushing off some dust.

"Really? San, is it true? You found a good spot?"

I nodded, lowering the backpack. "There were places to hide, and it looked surprisingly comfortable," I said. In the end, I hadn't actually witnessed Mr. Arai letting Sansho out of the bag. I'd waited a little distance away, pacing over tree roots and vaguely imagining I could evade some of the responsibility.

Kitae continued to look mournful even once we were all back in the car. As I gripped the steering wheel, I could hear her sniffing and Mr. Arai murmuring something in a low voice, but I couldn't make out what he was saying.

•

"I don't want fritters tonight," I said as soon as I got home. I'd been trying to think of what I could put between me and my husband, but I hadn't come up with anything.

"Oh. Why?" my husband said languidly. He already had the pan on the stove and was prepping the food with long chopsticks in hand as usual.

"It makes me feel fuzzy."

"There's nothing wrong with that."

"When I get fuzzy we can't talk about anything important."

My husband dipped the tips of the chopsticks into the bowl of egg-and-flour mixture, and flicked them over the hot oil. "There's no need to talk about important things when we're at home, is there?" he said.

"Then when are people who stay at home supposed to talk about them?" I said quickly. I had to face it today—I had to question him before I lost my human form.

But the more anxious I felt, the more sluggish my husband seemed to become. "The thing is, San," he said, adjusting the heat on the stove. "You keep saying we need to talk, but is that even true? Maybe you'd *like* to talk about important things. But do you have anything important to say?"

I started to feel less sure of myself. I focused on feeling strength in my stomach. "What about having children? It kind of got put on hold, and we haven't mentioned it since. How do you feel about it?"

"How do *you* feel about it?" he said, and I found myself at a loss for words. "See, San? There isn't really anything you want to talk to me about, is there?"

"What about your ex-wife?" I said in desperation. But I knew as soon as I said it that it wasn't a conversation I particularly wanted to have.

"You're like me, San. You don't really want to think about anything, and there's no need to pretend that you do," my husband said, and took one of the ginger shoots lined up on the cutting board and dropped it into the pan. "We don't want to have to face the big stuff, you and me. That's why being with you is so easy."

You're wrong, I wanted to say, but I couldn't get the words out.

"How could you have lived like this for four years otherwise?"

A shiver went down my spine. *Like this.* What was he trying to say?

"These past four years, did you ever once say you wanted to go out and find work?" my husband said in a syrupy voice, still gazing into the foaming pan.

A quail egg plopped its way into the oil.

"What did you think when you found out I already owned an apartment?"

Another egg went in.

"I knew from the start you'd never leave this place."

His voice wasn't my husband's. But I could no longer recall how my husband's voice sounded.

"I think you understand it all, San. Why you married me, and why I married you."

I felt the hairs on my body stand on end.

As I opened my mouth to scream, I felt something hot fall into it. "They're best eaten hot."

It was hot. So hot I thought I was about to burn myself. But the more I told myself I had to spit the fritter out right away, the more my mouth huffed and my tongue moved to taste it. The delicate aroma of in-season gingerroot rose to my palate.

"It's okay, it's okay. It'll start to taste good soon."

My husband looked at me.

His face, which I hadn't seen in a long while, was a perfect half-and-half mixture of my husband and me.

My husband continued throwing ginger shoots and quail eggs into my mouth, one after the other. It was horrifying, but also delicious. As I moved my mouth to keep up with the onslaught, the taste started to change into something I knew well.

"You thought you were the only one feeding yourself to me?" he said, twisting his body into a coil and smiling thinly. I cried out and tried to peel him off me, but it was too late.

I couldn't breathe. But the sense of revulsion gradually lessened, and soon enough, with tears in my eyes, I was filling my mouth with the familiar substance. "It's good, it tastes so good," I said, coiling, and breathlessly continued to revel in the taste of the thing I knew so well.

•

We ran into Mr. Arai just once after that, at the entrance to the apartment complex.

Mr. Arai, who was collecting his mail from the mailroom, stopped as soon as he spotted me and my husband, and said, "Oh!"

"It's been a while," I said, and bowed lightly.

"I see," Mr. Arai said, looking at the two of us in turn. "You decided against placing something between you."

"Yes. I felt that we could make it work without that."

"You weren't so averse to it, then."

"I guess not."

"I see. I see." Mr. Arai nodded again, and looked up at my husband, who was listening to our exchange suspiciously. "Well, there are plenty of very similar married couples out there. You're right. Perhaps it does work," he said, and walked off briskly toward the east wing.

I wanted to ask him what we looked like to him, but I watched him go in silence. Not long after that, Kitae told me that the two of them had decided to move back to San Francisco.

It was October, and several out-of-season typhoons made landfall in quick succession. People were saying it was because there had been so few during September that we were getting them now.

My husband had gotten a doctor's note and taken paid leave from work, and, providing me with the couch and highballs and the TV, took on the housework with a kind of relish.

That day, the biggest typhoon of the year was forecast to approach. Drops in air pressure triggered my migraines, so I'd been in an especially bad mood since morning. I started drinking earlier than usual to compensate.

"I went shopping on the main street today," my husband said after dinner.

"Uh-huh," I said from the couch, not really listening. Thanks to the painkillers I'd taken for the migraine, on top of the fritters I'd stuffed myself with yet again, my head felt even fuzzier than normal. Watching from behind as he eagerly folded the laundry, I thought, *He's finally progressed to shopping at the local shops.*

"The butcher's was closed. Apparently the owner fell sick last week? The old greengrocer said so."

"Hmm," I said. I'd heard about that only the day before yesterday myself.

"And our dry cleaner's going to be changing hands soon."

I knew that too. My husband noticed that my glass was empty, and got up smoothly and brought me a refill. What an attentive wife he was.

He waited quietly until I'd taken my first sip, and then continued. "Zoromi's cat food's going up next month. By sixty yen!" he said triumphantly.

But this was information *I*'d told him yesterday. *Caught you out*, I thought uncharitably, and looked at my husband, who had sat back down in front of the laundry. "Eighty yen, not sixty."

When I corrected him, my husband simply repeated himself. "Zoromi's cat food's going up next month. By eighty yen!"

He has no shame. "Only housewives understand what it's like to run a household," I said, taking a big swig of my highball. But my husband was pretending not to have heard. He was spreading a bath towel and demurely folding one corner to another. *Utterly shameless*, I thought again.

"You wouldn't know anything about being a housewife," I said, raising my voice without meaning to. My husband, who was sitting flat on the wood floor, kept his hands moving, folding the laundry assiduously.

"There's no point in clinging to me like this," I said to my husband's back. "It only relieves the suffering a tiny bit. It doesn't get rid of the temptation. I think you may as well give into it already, actually. What's the point of killing yourself trying to keep up the appearance of being human?" Letting the headache and the alcohol loosen my tongue, I hurled my real feelings at him. The words seemed to spew out of me in a torrent, in exact proportion to the amount of fritters he'd forced me to eat.

"You only say that to try to trick Husband!" My husband, who still had his back to me, suddenly emitted a screeching, high-pitched voice I'd never heard before from somewhere around the nape of his neck.

I was speechless with shock.

"I can tell. You're going to leave me because you've gotten tired of me, aren't you?" He was speaking in a peculiar tone, and I wondered whether he was trying to sound like me. His back started to quiver, and then the back of his head moved strangely, and, as though I were watching fast-forwarded footage, his short hair started to grow, furling and unfurling. Like inchworms crawling, the squirming tips moved as one mass toward his shoulders, copying the length of my hair.

"Why do you want to be the wife that badly?" I said. "Don't turn into me. Be something better!"

My husband finally stopped folding laundry. I saw his ears twitch like the ears of some wild animal.

"Husband! Go be a creature of the mountain!" I commanded.

His body started to shake violently, as though it had completely lost its shape. Its outline blurred, and his back ballooned up to double its size and then shrank down until it was much smaller, over and over. But he still refused to turn around so that I could see his face, and, struck with terror, I decided I had nothing to lose. I shouted, "You can stop being husband-shaped now. Take whatever form you want to be!"

The distending body of my husband exploded with a loud pop. It settled to the floor in countless small clumps.

I switched off the TV and gingerly peered over toward the laundry, where the clumps had fallen.

"Oh!" I cried out.

A single mountain peony was blooming behind a stack of bath towels. It had translucently fine white petals, and looked nothing at all like my husband.

I never knew he wanted to be such a dainty creature. My eyes were wide with surprise at its delicateness.

As the only proof that it had once been my husband, the mountain peony's stem was growing straight out of a pair of his underwear.

A married couple was a strange thing. Although we'd lived in such close proximity and spent our days and nights together, I hadn't had the faintest inkling that my husband's desire had been to be a single bloom of a mountain peony.

After daybreak, I took the mountain peony back to the mountain.

I planted him in a quiet, sunny spot near the rocky clearing where we'd set Sansho free, next to a purple gentian that was in bloom, so he wouldn't be lonely.

Back at the apartment, I made myself breakfast, washed a single set of dishes, did one person's worth of laundry, ran a bath for one, and got into bed.

When I closed my eyes, I sensed my fuzzy contour clamoring to reconstitute itself. *This is all mine?* I touched my still-humming body and felt amazed.

The following year, in late spring, I went to see my husband, who had turned into a mountain peony.

My husband was in bloom, vivaciously displaying a white flower, as pretty and unafraid as a paper lantern. Moved nearly to tears, I gazed for a while at his beautiful form. The gentian at his side, not to be outdone, was also flowering elegantly.

I lingered there, contented, until I felt ready to leave. I got up slowly and noticed that the two flowers looked very much like each other. As I examined them more closely I started to feel a chill, and I fled from the rocky clearing and left the mountain without looking back.

Paprika Jiro

THE FIRST TIME PAPRIKA JIRO SAW IT HAPPEN, he was ten years old, helping his grandpa with his greengrocer's stall in the market. Jiro worked hard, calling out to customers to buy their fruits and vegetables, so that he could contribute to his family's meager income. When he made a sale, he had to step on a wooden crate to reach the hanging basket where they deposited their earnings.

Grandpa's knees and hips weren't what they used to be, and he rarely got up from his barrel these days, but Jiro was the apple of his eye, and customers never failed to compliment him on what a fine grandson he had.

Other stalls in the market kept animals in cages to draw in customers, so Paprika Jiro did his best to compete by singing out the names of the fruits and vegetables in his clear boy soprano. His voice made people stop and listen, and brought a smile to their faces. He was going to inherit the stall one day. It should have been his dad, but he was a ne'er-do-well who drank.

It was the end of another day. Grandpa laid a gentle hand on Paprika Jiro's head.

"Time to be getting home?"

"Yes, Grandpa."

That was when they turned up.

Jiro heard a woman scream, and looked up and saw something approaching from the other end of the market, setting off what looked like fireworks of fish and meat and flowers, destroying stalls left and right.

Jiro gaped at the sight until he was startled into action by the cries of confusion and panic from the people around him. *They're here! They're back!*

"Come on, Grandpa, let's go!"

Jiro tugged at Grandpa's sleeve, but Grandpa didn't budge. Jiro brought him his cane, but Grandpa wouldn't take it. The ground rumbled as the thing approached, blowing up stalls and gathering speed. There were distant sounds of gunfire.

Jiro asked Grandpa why he wouldn't move. Grandpa smoothed his frantic grandson's head again, and said, "Getting chased on purpose, those folks, just to wreck our stalls."

Jiro didn't understand. An Asian man making kung-fu-type movements and a pretty white woman hurtled past in a tangle of legs. The man lost his balance and barreled headfirst into Grandpa's stall. All too easily, the wheels came off, and with a loud noise the stall fell on its side. The basketful of coins they'd worked all day to collect spilled and rolled away.

The man leapt neatly to his feet, and he and the woman ran off, neither of them showing a speck of interest in the destruction of the stall. But Paprika Jiro had noticed how the man had lost his balance on purpose, even though there'd been nothing at his feet to trip over. The man and the woman had made sure there were vegetables flying into the air and then had exchanged a satisfied smile. Soon men in black suits came running after the two of them, shooting guns, and razed anything that was still standing, like a pair of clippers buzzing the hair off someone's head.

Once they were gone, the market people went about quietly picking up the debris scattered all over the street. No one uttered a word of complaint. It was as though they'd been hit by a tornado or some other natural phenomenon.

"Just another part of being a market trader," Grandpa said placidly.

•

In the years that followed, Jiro saw them come back, time after time, with no warning, to destroy the stalls and disappear. Grandpa was killed by a stray bullet from a man in black. When Jiro first took over the stall, he tried to improve it by borrowing a tarp from a friend to make a roof, but no sooner had he installed it than they began to fall from the sky. They bounced once off the tarp and then fell straight through it, reducing the stall to splinters. No matter where he moved the stall, they kept coming. As long as he continued to trade in open air, they found him. They were like an infestation of bugs crawling out of the woodwork.

Just once, Paprika Jiro managed to grab on to the hem of the trouser leg of the very last suited man just as he hit the ground.

"Why do you do this? . . . Who are you? . . . What did we ever do to you?" Jiro shouted, in English that he had memorized specially.

The man, his eyes hidden behind sunglasses, stood Jiro upright with surprising gentleness and rubbed away a streak of dirt from his face. Jiro felt his hopes rise—he would finally get some answers!—but the man just quirked both ends of his mouth up and then made a beeline for the big metal gong that hung from the ironmonger's stall.

When Jiro quit the vegetable stall to become the market's

pigeon seller, they returned immediately and liberated every last one of his pigeons before he could say a word.

The whole market accepted them as a fact of life. No one else wondered where they came from or where they were going. But Paprika Jiro wanted to know the truth. One night, he filled a big pot with glue and placed it in front of the stall. A few days later, when he heard a woman scream at the entrance to the market, he stripped naked and jumped inside.

Jiro waited inside the slimy pot of glue, pinching his nose and holding his breath. The sounds of chaos gradually got louder, until he heard something break nearby. One of them thundered toward the pot where Jiro was hiding and smashed straight into it.

Covered head to toe in glue, Paprika Jiro stuck to the back of one man in a suit and watched the market grow smaller and smaller behind him. Once they had cleared the village and entered the desert, the man gave a strange cry—*Er-hai!*—and ran as fast as the wind. Jiro discovered that what he had assumed to be a dark business suit was actually just skin that looked like a suit. Even the sunglasses were part of the man's body.

Gradually, a group of large-breasted women and well-muscled men gathered behind Jiro, in a line that trailed into the distance. Their numbers swelled and swelled. They fired their guns wildly as they ran, and retrieved and ate fruits and vegetables they had somehow taken from the market from the inside pockets of their skins. When night fell, they ran even faster.

Eventually the glue peeled, and Paprika Jiro fell off into the desert. It took him seven days and seven nights to get back to his village.

Paprika Jiro remains a market trader today. These days he sees them less and less often.

"Because no one really believes in them anymore," says the ironmonger.

Once in a while, they still come through. Just like old times: in high style, in a cloud of dust and mayhem. As a mark of utmost respect, Paprika Jiro does his best to react in exaggerated astonishment as they careen through, fearlessly confronting obstacles head-on.

How to Burden the Girl

WHAT WAS I THINKING, GETTING INVOLVED with a girl like her? The only reason I was interested in the first place was that I thought she was an innocent young thing standing up to an evil gang all on her own. I had no intention of getting mixed up in such a violent love affair.

"You said you'd do anything to get to know me," she said, inching closer again.

I'd said that, sure. But I was thirty-four. I was dubious about my chances of understanding someone so much younger than I was, and anyway I know nothing about women. I'd just thought she must be lonely, what with her entire family having been killed by an evil gang, so the words had just slipped out. There was no need for her to take them seriously.

She moved slowly toward me. She'd just blown the heads off nineteen evil henchmen. I watched her closely while I retreated. I looked at the tears of blood she was crying because her beloved father had just become the last of her family to die, killed in a manner so diabolically cruel as to seem beyond human imagining. The special tears were the whole reason the gang was after her. I didn't know the details. I'd simply been taken by the way the girl's thighs looked, sticking out of her skirt. The pink hair, the emerald-green eyes—those were a little freakish, admittedly, but they didn't bother me. I'd thought some of them must just come like that. My old man would cry and sigh and call me a hopeless ignoramus if he knew. My mother walked out on the two of us a long time ago, so he's all the family I've got.

I kept creeping backward, and before I knew it, I'd left the living room. My foot came up against the staircase in the hall. Her house was enormous. She, her father, and her five brothers had moved here sometime last year, settling into a quiet life next door to the house I've always lived in. It looked like the girl's father took care of all the errands and things in the huge house behind the high wall, so at first I was simply excited to know there was someone next door in the same situation as I was. I rarely feel any curiosity toward other people, but I took to watching her through the windows occasionally, and would see her taking really good care of her five little brothers. This made me feel pretty inadequate. I leave all my cleaning and laundry to my old man. His stuff I leave up to him too.

At some point, I started to find it strange that she never left the house. What's more, the five little brothers, who looked so alike they could have been quintuplets, seemed to be disappearing one by one. I mean, one day there were only four boys playing in the garden; then there were three; then two. The little brothers carried on tumbling around the garden looking carefree, but on the days just after one had vanished, the father would usually come out and hold the girl's hand as she sat in a chair on the deck. On those days she'd forgo her usual bare legs and cover up in a dark outfit, looking glum. But why no funeral? Why no police?

One night, I saw one of the little boys nearly get snatched by members of an evil gang. I knew that that was what they were because their getup was pretty unmistakable: masked faces, capes, in black from head to toe. The girl and her father were fighting them off in their garden—him with a gun, and her with the kind of long sword I thought existed only in movies. (People around here pay no mind to moderate amounts of noise or gunfire, because there's a massive ballpark around the corner; their hearing's shot.) I was taken aback by the girl's almost superhuman physical ability. Her father looked realistic enough, like a man holding a gun, but the skill with which she wielded her sword as she killed those henchmen was way out of the ordinary. I should have realized then that she was different from your average woman, but what can I say? The only person I could compare her to was my old man.

They managed to save the little kid from being taken that day, but a few days later the gang came back and killed the kid in a gruesome fashion. That was my first sight of her tears of blood. The gang members held her down and used a dropper to collect a few tears into a vial and disappeared into the woods behind the house with a purposeful swirl of their capes. The garden was littered with the bodies of the little boy and numerous dead henchmen. Then there was the girl, sitting on the ground, clutching grass. And her father, coming up to her and gently putting his hand on her shoulder.

I started to piece the situation together. The gang was after her (for whatever reason), and it was no use trying to run (because they'd catch up at some point), so the girl and her father were trying to force a showdown next door. That much I got. I did think maybe their plan was in a little bit of a rut, what with the way the gang seemed to insist on attacking the house repeatedly instead of just taking the girl hostage, or the way she and her father let the little boys roam around for the taking when they could have been kept out of harm's way in a shelter somewhere. But I don't like to sweat the details.

That being said, if it had occurred to me, surely it had occurred to her—that once all the little brothers were dead, her father would be next. Reduced to just the two of them, the girl and her father expanded their arsenal and kept their guard up around the clock. It's possible they were staying put because they were using the father as bait, to lure out the evil gang and eradicate them once and for all instead of trying to find their HQ.

Their epic daily battles racked up mountains of dead henchmen, until one day it all came to an end. Her father was finally taken down.

The gang took just one drop of her blood tears and left, as usual. The girl sat on the lawn and wept. Her father, who'd always been there to hold her hand, had been blown to smithereens. Seeing how she was suffering, I was moved—despite not being in the habit of empathizing with people—to pop on a pair of sandals and make my way over to the stately and by-now-familiar garden next door. I entered the grounds through a segment of wall that had been damaged in the fighting. When I got closer to her, I saw the grass where she was sitting was entirely slicked with red. These were the tears whose mysterious powers the gang was after.

She didn't even raise her head as I approached. What do you do to get a woman to stop crying in a situation like this? "Chin up, now," I said, trying to keep the squeak out of my voice. I told her that I understood how she felt losing her last living relative. That I had no one besides my doddering old man.

I thought I might be in love. As she raised her face, I saw a red tear trail down her cheek and knew I'd do anything to take her father's place as her right-hand man. I didn't know how to shoot a gun, but perhaps I could learn to drive instead. I hardly recognized myself. I knew what this was called: unconditional love. The gang would probably be after me, but being beside her, even just briefly, would be worth it. My very first experience of love for a fellow human being. I'd bare my heart to her, tell her everything. How I've never been able to sympathize with anyone before, but would try to understand the loneliness that must come from having extraordinary abilities. That we'd no doubt face plenty of obstacles, but hey, there's always my old man.

She'd been still for so long, but suddenly she got to her feet. "Love?" she said, moving toward me, head angled inquiringly. "Love? Love? Think you'll still love me once you've heard what I've got to say for myself?"

I didn't know why she was acting so aggressive toward a guy who was obviously trying to help, but I figured she was probably confused.

"Nothing you can say will shock me," I said, affecting calm, nodding like a man of the world. I hadn't brought up my spying on her, but it was possible she'd been aware of me for some time.

"All this is my own fault," she said, "for falling in love with my father."

I was dumbstruck.

She looked into my eyes to make sure I was listening, and began her tale.

"I was ten years old when Mother first suspected I had designs on Father. She kept warning him, but he always brushed her off, told her not to be absurd. Said she had a bee in her bonnet. That I was only a child.

"But Mother was right. I meant to take him away from her. I used every trick in the book to turn them against each other. They'd been so close, but Father defended me until the very end, saying it didn't do to suspect a child. He wasn't interested in knowing the truth. He wanted to think of his daughter as some kind of angel. He should have realized that was hopelessly naive, if he remembered anything about being ten himself."

She stepped toward me, holding out her little hands. I should have been thrilled, but my body felt all tense, looking for a way to escape.

"Mother seethed, grew hysterical. Unable to prove that I was a wicked child, she finally cracked and shouted at me, and raised her hand in anger. That was the moment I'd been waiting for. I stumbled hard on purpose, and fell into the road. I was taken to the hospital and had to have a dozen stitches, but after that the court made sure she could never see me again. Father, who'd adored her gentle nature, divorced her, and we moved away together. Do you see? I got the law on my side.

"That's why Mother joined the evil gang. She needed to

find something that was more powerful than the law. I'm sure she made a study of every conceivable means of murder, purely to make me suffer—you know about the wonderfully imaginative, almost artistic ways each of my brothers was killed. You couldn't do that without a genuine love of killing, or a serious obsession."

She gave me no time to respond.

"One other thing—those weren't my little brothers. They were our children. Mine and Father's. I could hardly go to a clinic, so I gave birth to them all at home, in the kitchen. I admit I was pretty surprised when the triplets turned up. This isn't a fight for justice," she said, pausing at last. "It's a deeply personal matter."

I tried to rouse my stiff tongue. "But aren't they collecting your tears?" I said. "Those tears of blood, I thought they had some kind of special power."

"The tears?" She shrugged. "Who knows? They don't do a thing. Mother just takes them as trophies of the misery she causes me, drop by drop."

I'd obviously gotten everything wrong. What with the pink hair, and the fact she was just a girl, I'd simply assumed she was a plucky young thing fighting on the side of good. I wanted to get away, but as she kept trying to come closer, I'd inched my way back over the deck, and found myself inside the house.

•

"Do you really love me?"

She sounded sweet, but I no longer felt like saying yes. "I should really go check on my old man," I said, gesturing vaguely toward my house. "He hasn't got anyone but me to look after him."

She seemed to sense the advantage was hers. Grabbing my arm, she said, "If you love me, then find out how it feels to be me."

"How it feels?"

"To lose your family. You try it."

I'd realized a while ago that I was in over my head. But it wasn't going to be easy to get off the hook. I couldn't let my smile slip just yet.

"Lose my family? I couldn't kill my old man," I said.

"That's not what I mean. To feel what I feel," she said, immobilizing me with one hand, "you need to seduce him."

"I need to—"

"If you want to get to know me."

"But I'm—"

"That's what you need to do."

I hadn't been lying when I'd said I wanted to understand her, but there was no way I was going to seduce my geriatric father. Just picturing it made acid rise in the back of my throat.

"Aside from Mother, no one realized that I'd seduced Father, not even Father himself. He was full of guilt for having ruined my life, and I planned to use that to make sure we went on living together like man and wife. With Mother legally out of the picture, there was nothing to stop me from lying to everyone else, and taking the secret of my wickedness to the grave. Or so I assumed.

"But I was wrong. Because then it all started. First my hair: I used to have beautiful black hair. But soon it started to turn pink from the roots out. I dyed it, but it wouldn't take—when I woke up the next day the pink color would be deeper than ever. That wasn't all. It grew out at an incredible rate. I always wore my hair in a bob, but now it comes down to my waist. Eventually I gave up cutting it, because it just keeps growing.

"Next was my eyes. Each time I looked in a mirror, my irises had lost some of their dark color, until they were finally emerald green, like a doll's. And then my brothers. I told you they were mine and Father's children, but the thing is, we only ever conceived the first one. The rest of them we don't recall making. So all we were doing was living together, but my belly kept swelling, and I was trapped in a hell of perpetual morning sickness and contractions. Then, when I was giving birth, the babies' little heads would get caught, putting me in agony. Some of them got stuck for too long, and they didn't make it.

"I was gradually starting to understand what these changes meant. There was some force out there that wasn't going to let me get away with what I'd done to Father, even if I'd managed to fool everyone else.

"Soon I couldn't even leave the house, thanks to my outlandish appearance. In the early days, we kept moving from one place to the next, but every time we did, I got pregnant with another one, so we decided we'd go somewhere new, buy a house, and stay put. Once we got here, my perpetual pregnancies finally let up. We breathed a sigh of relief, thinking we might be forgiven at last.

"But there was another change yet to come. You know what I'm talking about?"

I said the first thing that came to mind. "The tears?"

"That's right." She nodded, still clutching my arm. "I started to cry tears of blood."

Was this some kind of sick joke? I was too confused to work out where her lies started, or how exactly she was different from other women. I mean, they were all completely foreign to me to begin with. I tried to pry her hand off my arm. She wouldn't let go, and kept on talking, as though she were trying to unburden herself by confessing everything. It was infuriating. I kicked her in the gut as hard as I could, and in a mad scramble half leapt, half tumbled down into the garden, clambering toward the shadowy darkness.

"Seduce your father!" I heard her cry. "Then you'll know what I'm talking about!"

I'd meant to aim for home, but I found myself in the woods behind her house, through which the evil gang always made its exit. I ran and ran, but the trees went on forever. There was no way it could be so vast. "Father! Father!" I shouted, but maybe he didn't hear—there was no sign of anyone coming to help. I saw that I was surrounded by countless mounds of soil, where the girl and her father had buried the gang members they'd killed daily. There were capes and masks scattered everywhere. Farther on, I came across five secluded graves.

After a while, I finally spotted the lights on in my house. I went to my room and slipped quietly into bed. The next day, my old man brought me some lunch. The moment I clapped eyes on him I remembered the night before, and promptly lost the will to eat his food. I couldn't bring myself to even speak to him.

The Women

THERE WAS NOTHING TO BE DONE. NO MATTER how many times I asked why, all she would tell me was that she was challenging me to a duel. I begged her to reconsider, but it was no good. She was the kind of girl who would call me every night when we first started going out just to check that we were really dating, a lover who was so slender she looked like she might break if you embraced her. I couldn't believe it.

She stood up, as if to say there was nothing more to discuss, and asked if I'd like to do it by the river.

"How did we get here?" I cried. "Could we choose a more romantic location, at least?"

She paused to think, and then started listing places that were special to us: The amusement park. The movie theater. The park with the unusual swings. The petting zoo. Our parents' homes. The courtyard at the college where we'd met . . .

"The river's fine by me," I said.

She nodded. "Anywhere much farther and we'll have to drive, which will be fine for getting there, but could be tricky on the way back," she said. Of the two of us, I was the only one who drove.

My suggestion that we wait until it got dark was rejected. Her excitement seemed to mount as we searched for the perfect spot along the river. I stole a glance at her profile and saw that her upper lip was curled back, exposing her teeth. I'd had no idea she felt so passionately about fighting me.

"I just want to know why," I said again, in tears.

She was breathing heavily. *Huh huh huh huh.*

Another man came over the bank, led by his girlfriend. He also had tears rolling down his face. For a second, I thought an enormous mirror had appeared in front of us. The girl reminded me of my girlfriend: she was short and energetic-looking, with an attractive face. The man was like me. Nervous and pale, with a wan air.

As we passed each other, I noticed something that took me by surprise. The girl was holding what looked like a dog's leash, the other end of which stretched up to the top button of the man's shirt. I tried to pretend I hadn't noticed it, but I couldn't help myself from looking at the collar around his neck.

"No good spots back there?" the girl said. She may or may not have noticed me staring.

"We've only just come out ourselves. We weren't sure which way to go," my girlfriend said. She was still panting. *Huh huh huh.*

"Same here," the girl said. "We just decided to follow the river." The two of them moved toward each other and started exchanging information, making it seem like the man and I should probably be talking to each other too.

"Hello," I said, and nodded exploratively.

For a second I was worried he couldn't understand me, but the man in the dog collar looked at my drying tears and, in a surprisingly normal voice, said, "So it's happening to you too." He wore glasses, and would have looked like a trustworthy office worker if not for the wrinkles in his suit. I didn't know how to react. Because the girl was a few steps away, the leash was now pulled taut, making it even less possible to ignore the collar around his neck.

"What has?" I said.

"You're the same as me," he said.

"What are you talking about?"

"Am I right in thinking you've been challenged to a duel?"

I looked over at our girlfriends in alarm. So that girl was also about to . . .

"Shh. Play dumb!" He admonished me without taking his eyes off my face. He sounded sharper than I expected. Maybe he had a position of authority at his company, in spite of the dog collar. "It's our fault," he said quickly, moving only his mouth as though the rest of his face had turned to stone.

Your fault? I almost asked, except I sensed he meant to implicate me when he said the fault was ours.

When I didn't say anything, he continued, "Didn't you wish for a more exciting lover? This is all because of the desires of men like us. The women—" There was a sharp pull on the leash, and I saw the light disappear from his eyes as he turned to plod after his girlfriend.

After that, we met many similar couples. All the men walked three steps behind the women, with sad expressions and heads bowed as if they were accepting heavy punishments. As we passed each other they signaled mutely to me with their eyes.

The women were starting to salivate. My girlfriend was walking in front of me, and I couldn't see her face, but I could hear the occasional watery dribbling sound, so I presumed that it was happening to her too. I had the impression her body was expanding. Her dress—one of her favorites, which she'd worn on some of our dates—looked uncomfortably tight. Her breath was getting faster and more rhythmic. *Huh huh huh huh huh.* Her spine was slowly arching as though it were being pulled by an internal spring. And to think she'd once had perfect posture, and had always looked after her appearance, from her shoes to her meticulously trimmed bangs!

"You're doing this . . . because of me? For me?" I asked, but she had her nose in the air and was busy sniffing something upwind. She seemed in no condition to talk. Decisively, I stepped in front of my lover and looked into her face. I couldn't have been more shocked if she'd punched me. Her eyes, which tended to droop demurely, were angled sharply upward, and her eyelashes had grown preternaturally thick and voluminous. A dark line rimmed her eyes and made her seem to be glaring at everything. It made me shiver. What a provocative look! And her mouth too: at first I thought she'd bitten through her lip by accident, but no. The pink was gradually flushing to a striking red. I reached out and brushed my finger across her lip. The color came off on my finger. It was lipstick. Her lips were producing their own lipstick.

She started making a strange gesture. She was desperately trying to hold down her chin, which kept rising. "You want to pull your chin back down?" I asked, and her eyes wordlessly answered in the affirmative. Using my thumb and index finger, carefully, to avoid breaking her delicate jaw, I tried repeatedly to push it down. But her jaw pointed resolutely upward, immovable. There was nothing more I could do. It was my favorite of her angles. It accentuated her beautiful neck and flattered her already-slim face. She cried out with an animal sound.

"What now?"

She was pulling the hem of her skirt down, and I tried to help her. The knee-length skirt of her dress was shrinking upward with incredible force. Stiletto heels were sprouting from the soles of her shoes.

"Not me," I said, shaking my head at her as she grimaced in pain. "I'm not that kind of man."

"Stop trying to defend yourself. This is what you wanted!" A man I didn't know yelled at me, and a flying rock grazed the side of my face. When I looked toward where the voice had come from, an old man was slowly getting backed into a corner by an old woman, who was wearing fishnet stockings and a skirt with a hem far north of her knees.

"We have to accept that we're responsible for the physical effects they're experiencing!" He bent to pick up another rock, and then made an appeasing gesture with his other hand to distract the old woman's attention.

"But why now? Why all of a sudden?"

"Sudden? Hardly. This could have happened at any point since humans first appeared on this earth."

"Exactly!" It was a young man sitting behind me, being stared down by a woman in a police uniform. "Life's not worth living if you're not tending to the whims and demands of a high-maintenance lover!"

Everywhere I looked, each and every woman was transforming into a legendary beauty of unbelievable gorgeousness. I turned to my girlfriend, still wiping off the lipstick that kept staining her lips.

"I know you were worried about my ex. It's true that being with her was exciting: I was always on tenterhooks. But I forgot all about her long ago. If you got the impression I found you in any way lacking, there's no truth to that at all."

Her black-rimmed eyes opened wider as she heard what I was saying. So she had been feeling insecure. Of course she'd never really wanted to duel at all. I continued to wipe off the lipstick.

"Don't change. I just want you to be yourself."

The old woman growled and leapt onto the old man. The old man shuffled and fell back. He held up his rock, but as he was about to strike, he stopped himself and slowly lifted both hands above his head.

The young people behind us had started too. I took my lover's hand in mine, and we resumed walking down the riverbank. The stilettos growing out of her shoes seemed to have given her the ability to move much faster and more dynamically. I thought she might have broken some of my fingers. I stopped us every once in a while to wipe off more of the lipstick.

She was no longer out of breath. Her nose was growing ever more beautiful in the light of the setting sun. Her eyes gave me chills. Her chin was held proudly aloft. Of all the women at the river, she was the most devastating beauty. I was continuously swabbing at the lipstick now, but I couldn't keep up. "I'm sorry," I said, crying again.

It came into view as we approached the bridge, a classic location for a duel: several hundred couples engaged in a melee defying all imagining. Battle cries rang out into the distance, screams, the clash of weapons, men begging for their lives from lovers who seemed beyond language, belated confessions of love . . .

"Don't change. I love you just the way you are," I said.

There on the riverside, with tears streaming down my face, I picked up a barbed wrecking ball from the ground near my feet and swung as though my life depended on it. My girlfriend leapt high into the air and evaded it easily, so I tossed the wrecking ball aside and ran into the river. She chased me with superhuman speed, even though the water came to her waist. Just as I thought I had reached the other side, she grabbed a fistful of my hair from behind and yanked it out of my head. A wail of pain escaped my mouth, but I managed to clamber onto the shore and acquire a stun gun from a man who almost mowed me down. When I looked back, my girlfriend was right behind me, coming at me with a ferocious expression I'd never seen before. I pressed the stun gun to her ribs and released the current. She opened her eyes wide and stumbled backward. I followed, maintaining the pressure of the gun against her body. She staggered and nearly fell. I was about to press the button again when she weakly said, "Stop. Please. No more. Help me."

Weeping, I swung at her head with a club I'd taken off a man I'd kicked to the ground. She fell back into the river with a splash, and drifted slowly downstream.

On the way home, I slowly recited the list of our special places. "The amusement park. The movie theater. The park with the unusual swings. The public petting zoo. Our parents' homes. The courtyard at the college where we met . . ."

I knew then that she'd let me defeat her. When I told her I loved her the way she was, it must have gotten through to her somehow. I couldn't stop crying. I walked past the old man, who had expired with his arms still outstretched in entreaty. My sweet, kind lover! I'd rather die than ever lose you.

Q&A

IN MY DECADES AS A COLUMNIST, I HAVE BEEN
honored to have had the opportunity to respond to the worries
and fears of so many women everywhere in the Q&A format, but
the time is fast approaching for this celebrated series to come to
an end. As you all may have started to suspect, I have reached the
limit of my living ability to blithely continue spouting phrases like
"your feminine radiance," or "a natural lifestyle," and so forth, not
only mentally but also on the purely physical level. As of this issue,
I am writing to you from a hospital bed.

When I expressed my desire to retire from this column, the editorial team was kind enough to ask me to reconsider. It's a reader favorite, they said; it's been running since our very first issue; you've made it this far, so you may as well make it your life's work; you still have a niche as a grandmother hot in pursuit of beauty beyond age. All much appreciated. Sadly, it is not within my power to live up to these kind expectations. However, in this issue, my last, the team has gone all out on a fifty-eight-page extravaganza of a feature, under the title "If You Can Do It, We All Can!" I myself intend to do my part by responding to as many of your questions as humanly possible. Without further ado, let's start with some from the editorial team: Thirteen Things We All Want to Know, But Thought It Was Probably Too Late to Ask.

Thank you, as ever, for reading.

Q. What do you think people think of when they think of you?

A. (1) Both men and women find me attractive; (2) I have a great deal of integrity; (3) My age, and the experiences that have come with it, have refined me as a woman; and (4) I keep my promises to family.

Q. Tell us about your thirties.

A. Having just made my start as a cover model for women's magazines at that age, and because of the media interest that went with it, I felt under pressure to say things that conformed to the image of a "desirable woman." My main memory is of women my age who welcomed me, as someone who had already borne and raised children, as a manifestation of the hope that they, too, could continue to enhance their feminine radiance. I enjoyed living up to everyone's ideal, and I believed I was doing a good thing. I probably had some innate talent for it, and soon enough I was in constant demand as a spokesperson and an arbiter of taste—a position that was cemented by my advice column, which first appeared in this magazine.

Q. What did you find difficult about being in the spotlight?

A. Expectations about me soared. I was someone who knew all there is of love. A connoisseur of the finer things in life. A woman who could take a joke. A lifestyle to aspire to. Style you'd want to copy. Frank views on sex. I could barely keep up.

Q. What's the total number of questions you've answered over your career?

A. Thousands? Tens of thousands? Even people I met in my private life couldn't help but spill their troubles to me within the first sixty seconds of our acquaintance. This magazine's main readership is women in their twenties and thirties, so most of the questions are about love relationships. Your concerns when it comes to love are much less unique and interesting than you imagine. The majority are variations on the following: How can I get the person I'm interested in to talk to me? He's having an affair. He won't have sex with me! My boyfriend is an asshole. And so on.

Q.   Problems that come with being an agony aunt?

A.   I started to feel that I was continuously giving advice in my daily life, whether I was getting my hair done, or having a meal, or walking a pet. If I was at lunch and dropped my knife under the table, I would ask myself, "Does the classy woman pick it up herself, or does she call a waiter?"; walking down the street, it would be, "Does the sexy woman turn left, or does she turn right?"; while having sex, "Does the woman of our dreams pursue her climax here, or does she wait?"

Q.   In your forties, you continued to be a leading figure in the world of women's magazines, and one of our most widely admired. However, on television, your somewhat unique voice and personality became the target of humor, inspiring jokes and widespread impersonation. How did you really feel about this?

A.   The imitations were malicious. They would trim their bangs into unnaturally straight lines, or try to outdo each other with the most pronounced lisp, or repeat comments that I had said just once as though they were catchphrases, to poke fun at them. I suppose it was gradually dawning on people that I was losing my way. And it was true—I didn't know how long I could keep going. I didn't know whether the world was trying to make me into a role model or a clown, and felt like I was walking a tightrope on an extremely precarious balance. I guess people were watching to see which side I fell on. As I was, myself.

Q. Your fifties?

A. I wasn't sure if my answers to people's questions were masterful profundities or the mad mutterings of an old hag.

Q. In your sixties?

A. I stopped caring.

Q. In your seventies?

A. Mad mutterings of an old hag.

Q. If you could give one piece of advice to your twenty-something self, what would you say?

A. Beware the pressure of having to represent the platonic ideal of an attractive woman! The constant tension of having to be ready to talk vivaciously about romance twenty-four hours a day, of exposing cleavage without flaunting it, of making sure to cross and recross your legs while wearing a short skirt. There will come a time when all your sex appeal can do for you is to make you want to vomit.

Q. How do you feel about the support you have enjoyed from women readers of all ages?

A. When so many people were doing impressions of me, and the prevailing culture came to see my existence as comical, it was only thanks to the support of my readers that I was able to escape being swallowed whole by the swirling torrents of malice. At that time, I felt I was desperately clinging to a small raft, and spent months in terror of capsizing. The muddy water only kept rising and rising. Many nights, I woke from the nightmare with a start, and jumped out of my bed in the dark to spit out the mud I could taste in my mouth. That I was able to regain my standing as though nothing had happened—no, even more, to further cement my place in the popular consciousness—once I had resigned myself to living as a clown: that was nothing short of a miracle. And I owe it to all of you.

Q. You've said, "I can only be me." Please share the source of your unshakable confidence.

A. When I had lost my way many times over, and didn't know where to turn, what I needed to do in order to find myself again was to let myself do an impression of myself. That's right. For a long time now, I've only been doing what everyone else was doing already—impersonating me. My mannerisms, my voice, the things I say—"What would I say *if I were me*?" "What would *I* do?" When what I really wanted to be was a tap dancer! But what does what *I* want have to do with anything? Other people made me into who I am. Isn't that actually far more glamorous?

Q. Do you ever still have doubts?

A. None whatsoever. Once I had made the decision to live and die with you all, my conviction never wavered. Even now, in my eighties, I still intend to continue to be "what every woman aspires to be," in both mind and in spirit, albeit from my sickbed.

Now, for the very last time, one of the most iconic columns in the history of women's magazines, and the culmination of my life's work: questions on life and love from you, my readers.

Q. I can't leave my boyfriend, even though he's physically abusive. (Nurse, 28)

A. Challenge him to a duel. Call him out to the river at midnight, and have at each other once and for all. In the face of your resolute blows, set free from the bounds of reason, he is unlikely to be able to resist picking up a rock. It may hurt, but that's where you'll need to be brave. You will find you already have what it takes inside you. Drift along the border between life and death for a while. Try to act very dead. He will probably be frightened into leaving the scene without checking whether you are or not. When he finally goes, take all the time you need to shiver with joy.

Q. I always end up waiting for him to call. (Aspiring home-maker, 23)

A. Long, long before we learned to wait for things like that, we were already waiting for something else. We've been waiting our whole lives for the moment when everything we can see vanishes in a puff of smoke, and someone claps their hands and says, "Your whole life up to now has been a lie. Your real life starts now." Which is to say that *he* is not the one leaving you hanging.

Q. I can't seem to meet the right person. (Office worker, 34)

A. It's about time you faced up to the fact that this is a thoughtless delusion. There's no way there isn't a right person out there for you. After all, aren't we all born right people? What I mean is, we all limit our own options too much. Have you considered someone from a different country? Someone old enough to be your father? Make a big change and try being with a woman. If you still can't find the right person, then try expanding your age range all the way down to newborn. Once you can include ten- and eleven-year-olds, the possibilities will only widen. Look into partners you may not have previously considered. Animals are good, as are inanimate objects. If you genuinely desire not to be alone, I recommend that you take a bicycle saddle as your next partner. You think that's out of the question? But a saddle is shaped surprisingly like a human face, and once you pull it off the bicycle, you can take each other out anywhere. When you go on vacation, the money you save on the second fare means you can make many more happy memories than if you were with another human. Best of all, a saddle can't speak. You lament that you can't find the right person because you have too many expectations of men who speak, and end up seeing too many of their failings. But if your partner is a bicycle saddle, there's just one thing you need from them: to gently and lovingly support your ass.

Your town is overflowing in opportunities for you to meet your future partner. How many bicycle saddles are lined up outside the train station, just waiting for you to choose them? Nothing is stopping you from going up to the bike parking, and, like the king of some small country, boldly selecting from their ranks.

It may happen that you fall for a saddle at first sight, only for its owner to throw a wrench in the path of your love. "Hey, you there, what do you think you're doing, trying to take my saddle?" Stand firm. Simply tell the owner that, while the saddle may as well be any of thousands for them, for you he is the only one in the world. If you suggest that the owner can take your saddle, the one you've never quite gotten along with, instead—be sure to carry it around with you for the purpose—then the majority of saddle-owners are sure to agree. Put your heart into it, and convey the depth of the love you feel.

Once you're finally alone with your chosen saddle, the rest is up to you lovebirds! Why not hold him by the stem as though he were walking alongside you, and skip down the sidewalk together?

He will never sniff dismissively as a human man would when you suggest going deer-watching for your next date. Even a movie in the most questionable taste will not elicit a yawn. Go to a museum. See the sights. Gaze over the city as it's lit up at night, and lean in close, and get a romantic mood going to rival any other couple.

Of course, there's likely to be the occasional jeer or heckle from an insensitive bystander, pointing out that your lover is a bicycle saddle, but let this minor obstacle only stoke the flames of your love. Your partner will no doubt be prepared to be swung as hard as it takes to protect your honor. More important, most human men are no match for his manliness in bed.

What do you say? Can't you just picture the charms of stepping out with a bicycle saddle?

If you and an attractive saddle end up embarking on a serious relationship as a result of this, please make sure to send in a photograph. I will certainly be delighted to participate in your wedding.

Editors' note: We have brought you a condensed version of our exclusive eight-hour-long hospital-room interview with the one woman you can't afford to take your eyes off this season—radiant as she continues to mature as an icon and a role model, still juggling home and career, giving her all to every question, as instructive as ever, right up to the very end. Her advice has attained the realm of the oracular.

The Dogs

I ONCE LIVED WITH A WHOLE LOT OF DOGS.

I don't recall their breed, which is strange, because we were close, and spent so much time together. I loved those dogs, and they loved me. There were dozens of them, each one bright white like freshly fallen snow. I spent my days warm and comfortable in a room with a fireplace, not seeing anyone. The dogs did ask to be let out, but I never once saw them doing their business—which was also strange, but at the time I assumed that they were modest and had set up some kind of toilet area away from the cabin. I didn't like beds, so I slept standing up, leaning against the windowsill. The dogs would gather around me at night like an overcoat, leaving only my mouth and eyes exposed. I enjoyed drowsily gazing at the fire, drifting to sleep, with the heady feeling of being engulfed by the mass of dogs.

At the time, I had some work that I could do holed up in the cabin. It involved sitting at the desk in the attic from morning to night, peering into a magnifying glass, tweezering tiny pieces of paper of innumerable colors: work too mind-numbing for most people even to contemplate. For many years, come winter, I'd take several weeks' worth of food and water and hide myself away in that cabin, which belonged to someone I knew.

The cabin consisted of a high-ceilinged living room, a small bedroom, and an attic, but that was plenty of room for me. When I first reached the isolated cabin, having driven inexpertly over the narrow, winding mountain roads, I was still on my own. I remember dropping the keys and struggling to pick them up again while still holding all my luggage, because the bulky scarf that covered half my face prevented me from seeing my hands. Autumn had just ended. Toward the beginning of my stay I'd definitely gone to sleep alone, looking out the window each night and feeling as if I were at the bottom of a deep sea. I don't recall when the dogs started living there.

I loved all the dogs equally. At first, I tried naming them one at a time, but I didn't get very far. I'd never actually liked naming things. I was content just looking into the glossy black of their eyes, which shone as though they'd been fired in a magic kiln. It wasn't as if the dogs called me by name, after all. But this got to be a little inconvenient, so I came up with names to try out on some of them. I lined up the dogs in front of the fireplace and told them to bark if they heard a name they liked. Then I held up the collars I'd fashioned and, looking into their eyes, called out the names one by one.

"First up, Early Morning."

Heh heh heh heh.

"The Day the Appliances Arrived."

Heh heh heh heh.

"Pastrami."

Heh heh heh . . . Yap!

The dog stuck his tongue out deferentially. I placed the collar marked PASTRAMI around his neck.

"The World."

Heh heh heh heh.

"Takeout."

Yap! Yap yap!

The dogs took care of their own meals as well. I surreptitiously let them out in the mountain woods, so they probably hunted animals as a pack. Once when I went for a walk among the trees,

I found what looked like a bird's skull at the bottom of a tree. I slipped the skull into my coat pocket and, when I returned to the cabin, I threw it at the dogs where they lay lounging. "Boo!" I shouted. The dogs didn't really react, but I thought that must be because they were ashamed that I knew they'd been eating birds. They never let me see them feed. What I did see them doing was drinking plenty of the very cold water that I got from the well behind the garage. I tried warming up milk and putting it out for them so they didn't catch a chill, but they wouldn't touch that. The ice-cold water seemed to energize them.

One day, I drove down the mountain to replenish some food supplies and came across a knot of people from the town, puffed up in woolly hats and down-filled jackets and gathered by the roadside.

I slowed down to see what was going on. Through the open car window I heard a voice saying something about a dog. My heart skipped a beat. The dog curled up in the passenger seat next to me began to raise his head as if he had sensed something, so I said, "Hush," and held his round head down in my hand. He'd come nosing around my feet as I was getting in the car, so I'd brought him along.

The dogs' heads just fit in the palm of my hand, and I was always moved by how their little skulls were wrapped in soft fur. This helped me stay calm on this occasion too, and I quietly rolled up the car window and slipped past the townspeople. Perhaps a dog had caused some kind of problem. In the supermarket, I kept my scarf wound twice around my neck as usual, hiding half my face, to discourage the staff from approaching me. But when the shop assistant from the fruit-and-vegetable section looked into my basket and casually remarked, "Stockpiling All-Bran again?" I plucked up my courage and asked, "Has something happened in town?"

The man looked a little taken aback—probably because I'd spoken at all. "A five-year-old boy's gone missing," he whispered.

"A child? Was it a kidnapping?"

"Kidnapping? No, nothing like that would happen around here."

"Then what?"

"Maybe he fell into the valley when his mother took her eyes off him."

The bantering air of familiarity that had arisen between me and the shop assistant became unbearable, so I hurried away with my cart. The dog, who'd apparently been asleep at the foot of the passenger seat, looked up at me blearily, and I gave his head a stroke.

I swung by the gas station. There was an elderly attendant there who would always try to strike up a conversation with me. I found it a bit of a trial, but it was the only gas station in town.

I didn't keep in touch with anyone. I'd always considered my only strengths to be that I was completely content not to talk to a single soul all day and that I had a high tolerance for monotony. The exception was the phone call I got once a week from a certain man. Of the few people I'd met over the years, he was the only one I felt I could still confide in. We had no romantic feelings for each other, simply a relationship where we could say what we honestly thought. When I heard his voice, my shoulders would let go of some of their tension, like the knot in a firmly tied silk scarf loosening deep inside a forest, far from where people are. His speech was distinct, like an oiled egg popping out of his mouth.

There was no doubt he was a misanthrope, like me, but unlike me he had enough courtesy and presence of mind not to let it show. He was the one who let me use this cabin, and would always joke that it was because he wanted me to pursue the life he couldn't. We often put our opinions to battle on the subject of whether it was better to distance ourselves from civilization or immerse ourselves in it, and when we tired of that we could hang up without a hint of awkwardness. He had a family. After our phone calls, I felt relieved at having fulfilled some minimal quota of human interaction, and comforted by the thought that he seemed to be making steady progress in the kind of life that was my "road not taken."

There wasn't a set time for our phone calls, but on that day, like on others, I had a premonition that made me look up from my magnifying glass. I must have been engrossed in the work—though I'd barely had a sip of my hot milk, five hours had passed since I'd come up to the attic. I put my tweezers down on their stand and got up from the chair, checking that none of the tiny pieces of colored paper were stuck to my hands or clothes. Above the desk there was a window with two layers of glass, and I could see several dogs running around in the snow outside.

I descended the ladder with the empty thermos and mug in one hand, and was warming up some more milk when the phone rang. Stirring the aluminum saucepan with a spoon, I reached over with my other hand and slowly lifted the receiver.

"Hey," he said. "I hope you're not suffering from isolation fatigue."

No, I said, and asked whether he wasn't suffering from socializing fatigue, to which he responded that of course he was.

"You settled in your burrow? Anything giving you trouble?"

I told him about mountain life—the hair dryer blasting out air that was unbelievably cold, the paths that got buried in snow despite constant shoveling, the front door that I had to hurl my body against when it jammed, the hunks of snow that fell into the fireplace and sent ash flying everywhere.

He said, "That's why I never go there in winter. I don't know how you stand it. After living like that, are you really going to want to come back down when spring comes?"

I informed him I'd been down to the town just that day, thank you very much, then asked him never to speak of spring again, because I didn't want to think about it. That brought the afternoon's events back to mind, so I told him about the huddle of townspeople I'd come across. "There might have been some kind of incident down there."

"An incident? Wonder what, in such a nowhere town."

I was reluctant to tell him more. I didn't want him to latch on to it and start looking it up in the papers or on the internet. I stopped stirring the saucepan and looked over to the dogs stretched out in the living room. Sprawled on the rugs like white sausages, they acted unconcerned, but I could tell they were a little unsettled by my being on the phone, like a jealous boyfriend. I guess my demeanor changed slightly during these phone calls. It occurred to me that I could ask him about them. Why hadn't I thought of this before? They might have been his dogs.

"Hey, about those little white fellows," I said.

"Those ones?" he asked.

"Yeah. They're doing really well."

There was a pause. "Oh," he said. "Here, not so much, but I did spot some of those little white fellows by the road today. Although maybe they weren't so white. Most of them are black now, with all the gravel and the dirt."

"Is that so?" I wondered whether black dogs were really more common in cities.

"Plus, the black fellows aren't doing so well. All melting and deformed, more or less on their last legs."

I cut off his laughter. "You really don't know?"

"Know what?"

He wasn't playing dumb. But for some reason now, I didn't find it strange in the slightest that he didn't know about the dogs. One of them came up to me and pressed his fluffy coat against my shin. I knelt down and rubbed his sides as if I was giving him a good scrub, and just said, "I'll tell you next time."

"Sure," he replied, as though to say he was used to my crotchety ways.

After that, we chatted about nothing in particular, and I got through two mugfuls of hot milk. As we were about to hang up, he asked whether I'd seen the weather forecast. I reminded him there was no civilization up here, and he told me, laughing, that a fierce chill would be invading over the weekend.

I decided to follow the dogs in secret when they went out to play in the woods. Once I was holed up in my workroom with the thermos, they knew I wouldn't be back out for a few hours, so they would start to disperse. They each had a favorite spot. Some liked to be just outside the door to my workroom, and others to lie on the clothes strewn around the bedroom and the living room, but most seemed to be happier outside.

I put on sunscreen to protect against snow burn, and some mirrored sunglasses and an anorak, and left the house. I traced the dogs' footprints through the bare trees, reveling in my afternoon stroll. Picking up a branch that I liked the look of, I drew mean-dering lines in the bright snow as I walked, occasionally swapping the branch for another when I encountered a better one.

The dogs' prints were almost always all in a bunch. They were basically toddling along the least arduous path. Every so often, a set of tracks diverged from the rest, but then shortly came back to rejoin the group. I thought they must hunt as a team, like wolves.

Before I knew it, I was on a path that I'd never been on before. I looked over to a clump of trees and saw one dog peeking through them from behind a bank of snow. His eyes were wide, and he was only visible from the nose up. I waved my branch number five, which was curled like a spring, removed my sunglasses, and said, "I followed you. Is everyone over there? May I join you?"

The dog got lightly to his feet and barked. Then he turned on his heels and ran off. I advanced into the clump of trees through knee-high snow, calling after him, "Should I not have come?" Feeling like a parent secretly checking on whether my children were doing their homework, and suppressing a grin, I looked out from behind a great tree.

I was astonished to see where they were: on a large frozen lake. I hadn't known it was here, but there the dogs were, stepping with a practiced air across the lake, which was big enough to hold sev-eral games of baseball at once. It was as if a ready-made dog park, sculpted by nature, had suddenly appeared before my eyes.

The dogs seemed to have no idea I was behind the tree, and

were scattered in all directions. I tried to get closer to see what they were up to, but the ice at the water's edge was thin, and far too treacherous. I stayed where I was and squinted at the dogs beginning to jump up and down. At first, they only jumped up about as high as they were tall. Gradually their time in the air seemed to increase, until they were jumping so high that they could have cleared the head of a person standing. It seemed that they were each trying to make a hole in the ice. Their front paws made digging movements, trying to break through the surface. Before long, each dog succeeded in making its hole, and jumped swiftly into the water. When the last one had dived in, they were nowhere to be seen. It was as if they'd melted away.

One of them poked its head out of its hole in the ice and sounded a short, sharp cry. *It's drowning and calling for help*, I thought in alarm, but in the next moment another dog stuck its head out of the freezing water in a different spot and made the same birdlike cry. More and more dogs popped their heads out from the ice, repeating the cry. It dawned on me what was going on. Swimming as a pack, the dogs were forming a large circle under the ice. And, using their cries, they were slowly closing the circle toward its center. I couldn't take my eyes off them. I walked around the lake, and when I found an area where the ice seemed thick enough to hold me, I leapt onto it. Using my gloves like windshield wipers, I scraped away the frost and peered through the ice.

The only thing I could see was gray muddiness at the bottom of the lake.

I made my way back to the cabin alone, picturing the dogs gracefully chasing fish through clear water.

That weekend, I woke to the morning I'd always wished for. Every last thing in the world seemed to have frozen over. The All-Bran I kept in the cupboard was in clumps so hard it was like eating hail, and seeing the icicles protruding from the roof I felt like I'd been transported overnight to a grotto filled with stalactites.

Once I'd put on as many layers as I could, shivering all the while, I took an empty bucket and shovel and headed to the garage. The dogs scampered around me, keeping close to my feet as if to hurry me along. By the time I reached the garage, taking three or four times longer than usual, sweat was pouring out of me as though I were in a sauna.

I made sure the generator's battery indicator was green. I checked how many liters of diesel fuel were left, then decided to dig out some more snow tools. I discovered some emergency tubes of chocolate, years past their use-by date. Finally, I took some old, dusty blankets and went around to the back of the garage. I looked down into the well, and a solemn chill plastered my face. The extreme cold had formed a miniature ice rink in there.

"What shall we do?" I asked the dogs behind me. "Can't get you any water."

The one with the collar marked PASTRAMI tried to climb up onto the well, scrabbling with his paws. "Get off!" I told him, and decided to do what I could about the frozen pulley at least.

I brought out a chisel and a mallet from the garage, and as I pounded like a blacksmith with all my might, the frozen rope finally started to give. I took hold of the rope with both hands and gave it a hard tug, and the layer of ice that had formed over the mechanism came away with a clatter as the pulley quickly began to turn.

That was when it happened. Pastrami leapt up onto the well, somehow got into the bucket, and disappeared down the hole, looking pleased with himself.

"Pastrami!" I shouted, but it was too late. He was yapping and rolling around in anguish at the bottom, having slammed onto the thick ice. Frantic, I worked the rope, raising and lowering the bucket that had fallen with him, trying to get him to jump back in it, but the bewildered dog could hardly stand up. "Go get help!" I called to the dogs crowded behind me. I heard the footfalls of several dogs running off. I leaned into the well and stretched my arm down, shouting, "Pastrami! Pastrami!" but the yapping cries reverberating up the well were overwhelming and I couldn't keep my eyes open.

When I came to, I was slumped by the edge of the well. Pastrami's cries had ceased, as had the sound of his forepaws scraping at the ice.

"What should I do if an animal jumps into the well?" I asked. The power lines had gone down under the weight of snow, and it was late at night before I got through to him on the phone.

"Animal in the well?" he said, a little sleepily.

"Yeah." I was wrapped in old blankets from the garage. I'd tried to keep my mind occupied all afternoon, chopping firewood and doing other things, but when night fell, I suddenly felt completely drained, and found myself unable even to stand up. The dogs had stayed close by me through the day, like watchdogs.

"Actually, I did find something like a weasel drowned in it once."

"Was it winter?"

"Summer."

"Then that's a different situation."

"I think I got someone from the town to get it out. I could give you the number. What is it? A raccoon?"

I told him that I couldn't really tell because it was all the way at the bottom. He suggested it might be dangerous, and that I should just put the cover back on and leave the animal there. Wolves sometimes prowled the area looking for food, he said. He would come by with his family on his next day off to take care of it. My mind kept replaying Pastrami trying to jump up into the well bucket, and I was terribly tired, so I told him that I wanted to go to bed now. "If you ever feel in real danger . . . ," he began, then went on to tell me how to unlock the cupboard in the bedroom, which he'd never let me touch before. The emergency hunting rifle was hidden in there. I told him I had no need for such a thing, and hung up.

I was checking that the drafty living-room window was properly closed so I could go to sleep, when I thought I heard the faint cry of a dog. I raised my head. Was it the wind howling? With a storm lamp and a shovel, and with the other dogs in tow, I made my way through the snow toward the well.

The bucket was rattling against the pulley as the wind blew. I stopped a few paces from the well and raised the lamp. "Pastrami?" I said in a small voice, almost to myself. "Pastrami?"

I thought I heard the keening cry of a dog in distress.

"Pastrami, are you alive?" I called again.

This time I could definitely make out the dog crying. I flung myself toward the well. In the lamplight I could see Pastrami, getting up on the ice! I left the lamp and the dogs, retrieved a chainsaw from the garage, and returned to the cabin. I sawed off the ladder that led to the attic, getting showered in sawdust, and loaded it on the red sled that I used for transporting firewood. Once I was back at the well, with the aid of some of the dogs, I lowered the ladder into the well, careful not to break the ice, and called the dog's name. I wanted him to take hold of the ladder somehow. But Pastrami only looked up at me with his tongue hanging out, and wouldn't make a move.

The ice at the base of the well seemed thick, and gave no sign of cracking when I tapped the ladder on it. I screwed up my courage and tentatively climbed over the edge, then gingerly stepped onto the ladder. Slowly, cautiously, I descended. Pastrami wagged his tail weakly as I approached. Just as I'd put one foot on the ice and reached for him, there was the slight cracking sound of something giving way, and all the blood drained out of my body. With bated breath, I coaxed the stone-cold hunk of fur down into the front of my jacket. I put my hand on the ladder to climb back up, but stopped short. The other dogs had surrounded the rim of the well and were staring down at us, motionless.

One dog moved its mouth clumsily just as the wind howled. I thought I heard the dog say, "Good enough."

Terrified, I found myself on the verge of laughter.

"Good enough?" I said. "For what?"

Beyond the still forms of the dogs looking down at us, I saw clouds being blown across the sky. Pastrami, who had been keeping still inside my jacket, yapped, as though remembering that he was a dog.

•

It was a pain having to go down the mountain, but my friend was adamant about keeping stocked on certain things. I made up my mind to go to town for the first time in a week. When I got to the garage, Pastrami was waiting beside the car door, looking fully recovered and eager to come along.

"No, stay home," I said. After what I'd seen last time, I thought it better to leave him behind. I drove down the mountain roads carefully, and saw that Christmas decorations were up all around town. It must be that time of year already. As I looked around, mulling over my long string of holiday-season social failures, I noticed that something was a little off.

It was people's expressions—they seemed haggard, somehow. Some were constantly glancing behind themselves in fear. An elderly person sitting on a bench had the puffy face of someone who'd been up crying all night. There were few cars on the road, and every house had its curtains drawn. Was I imagining it? Even the overly cheerful Christmas decorations gave the impression that the town was desperately trying to avert its eyes from something upsetting.

The shop assistant in the fruit-and-vegetable section wasn't around. Normally, I'd have been relieved, but this time it bothered me, so I asked the woman restocking the frozen foods what had happened. "Yes, that boy—he quit." Quit? All of a sudden? The woman gave me a long look. I thought I detected wariness and irritation in her eyes and quickly walked away. For some reason, the dog food had been moved, even though the cat food was still in the same place. I thought about asking where they'd put it, but I didn't feel like engaging that woman again.

The older man at the gas station with whom I always exchanged a few words wasn't there, either.

"Is he not working today?" I asked the young attendant in the Santa hat as he handed me my change. I'd gotten him to put a plastic container of diesel in the trunk for me.

"Mm-hm." He nodded ambiguously. There it was again. Each time I mentioned someone who wasn't there, I could sense irritation rise in the townspeople's eyes.

I was absorbed in a poster for a Christmas party—FORGET ALL YOUR TROUBLES!—when I felt the young man staring at me. "He said I could ask him if I ever needed anything. I was counting on it," I said, almost to myself.

"Let me know if there's anything I can do," said the young man, batting away the pompom on his Santa hat.

"Do you mean that? I might take you up on it." I hoped my eagerness to get back up the mountain wasn't showing on my face.

"Sure." He trotted inside to the cash register to bring me a pale pink flyer. "The charges for the services are all on here, if you'd like to take it with you."

I thanked him and rolled up the window, but one more thing was weighing on my mind. I rolled the window back down and asked offhandedly, "Do you deal with dogs?"

"Dogs?" he said. There was a pause, and he pointed at the bottom of the flyer. "You can see about dogs at the bottom there."

I stopped for a red light outside the police station. I was contemplating the sign in large print on the noticeboard—FOR THE GOOD OF THE TOWN, THEY'VE GOT TO BE PUT DOWN—when a huge truck behind me blasted its horn.

After that, I spent most of my waking hours at my desk, because I really had to knuckle down to my work. It required bottomless reserves of concentration. Several jobs were already complete and framed, and lined up along the attic wall, but even when I looked at those, I didn't understand in the slightest what made people want to pay so much for them. But there was no need for me to understand. The thing that mattered was that having this work let me avoid dealing with people. The thing was, the more progress I made, the more time I spent dreading when I would have to leave this place.

I was having a leisurely soak in the bath for the first time in a while, feeling good about the amount of work I'd gotten done, when it occurred to me that I hadn't had a phone call in a few days. When I looked at the calendar in the kitchen, I saw it was four days past Tuesday, when he always rang. I checked the time, which was only eight at night, and decided to ring him myself. No answer. No matter how many times I tried, I didn't even get through to the answering machine. Had something happened? He was conscientious, not like me. When he'd had appendicitis, he'd left me a message letting me know he'd be in surgery and wouldn't be answering his phone for eight hours—that was the kind of person he was. It could be that the phone had actually rung, many times, and I'd been too engrossed in the work to notice. I checked the calendar again, and was taken aback. It was December 31!

I decided to do something about the draft from the living-room window before the arrival of the new year. I got some putty and pressed it into the window frame. Then I noticed the pale pink flyer on the floor beneath the coat rack. I sat down on the sofa with the dogs and looked through the list of services available, just in case. The prices seemed a little high, but I could see myself calling them in an emergency. There was no entry for "Retrieval of animals in wells," although there was one for "Recovery of dead birds in chimneys." Farther down, the item "Dog walking" had been heavily crossed out. I recalled the exchange with the young man at the gas station. The last item on the list was even more mysterious.

"Extermination of dogs."

Perhaps they meant feral dogs, I thought as I stroked the heads of the white dogs. But surely that sort of thing would normally be left to the public health department. I suddenly remembered the strange snow tools, like big sharp forks, that I'd seen propped beside the winter tires at the gas station. What could they have been for? The dog I was petting pricked up its ears, barked menacingly, and leapt onto the flyer, ripping it to shreds. "Stop it!" I said, but then the other dogs caught the scent of the paper and, crouching down ready to pounce, started howling and growling as if they'd gone mad. *Yap yap, yap yap yap!*

I calmed them down, got up from the sofa, and thought about ringing him again. But for some reason, I already knew he wouldn't answer, and instead I dialed the number for my parents' place, for the first time in a long time. No one picked up, despite it being New Year's Eve. Just to make sure, I tried the police. No response. The fire department. No response. I dialed every number I could think of, but all I heard was the phone ringing, over and over.

I got my jacket from the coat rack, and with car keys in hand headed to the garage. The dogs followed and tried to get in the car. I told them I was just going down to have a look around the town, but this didn't satisfy them.

You want to come too?

Yap yap!

But I can't take all of you!

Yap yap yap! The dogs went on barking as if they were broken.

It took an hour to walk down to the foot of the mountain, white dogs in tow. When I got there the town was deserted.

There were still Christmas decorations everywhere. I heard

pet dogs crying from inside their houses, so I pried open the doors and let them loose, but the white dogs didn't respond to them in the slightest. The newly freed dogs ran off in a flash, as if to get away from the white dogs as quickly as they could.

I spent a long time wandering around the town, and ascertained that there wasn't a single person there. At the gas station, I found the words OUR TOWN sloppily spray-painted on a wall. *Our town.* I remembered that once, many years ago, I'd asked Santa Claus for a present: to wake up and have the whole world to myself.

I gathered as much food and fuel as I could carry, and headed back to the cabin with the dogs.

The following day, I sat and worked in the attic with the magnifying glass and tweezers, and went walking with the dogs over the snowy slopes when I needed a break. There was no sign of anyone approaching the cabin. I spent the next day the same way, and again the day after that. Watching the white dogs hunt, swimming gracefully under the ice, I could be engrossed for hours. When I ran out of food, I went down to the town and procured what I wanted from the unattended shops. I slowly became dingy and faded, but the dogs stayed as white as fresh snow.

One day, while I was watching them play in the snow from the attic window, I took the hunting rifle from the cupboard and let off three shots in their direction. The dogs stiffened in a way I'd never seen them do before, looked toward me, and then scattered into the mountain as though to meld into the glistening snow. The day hinted at the arrival of spring.

I leaned out the window and yelled, "Sorry!" at the top of my voice. "I won't do that again! Come home!"

That night, as the snow fell silently, I slept standing by the windowsill huddled with the dogs, who had come back. As I reveled in the sensation of being buried in their warm flesh, I thought, *I'll be leaving this place tomorrow.*

The Straw Husband

HER HUSBAND RAN LIGHTLY AHEAD OF HER, almost as if he were pacesetting a race. He was dressed in his favorite team's soccer jersey and knee-length shorts. His legs were sheathed down to the ankles in the compression tights they'd bought together at the sporting goods store, but from the gap between them and his sneakers, two or three strands of dry straw were poking out. The asphalt surface of the wide running track in the park was littered with sawdust-like material in his wake, but Tomoko skillfully avoided it as she tuned in to what he was saying.

"Good, nice and tall now. Try not to lift your feet—it's better to almost brush them forward just barely over the ground. You'll get less tired that way. Keep your elbows tucked in to your body. And don't stick your belly out."

"Okay," Tomoko said, wondering what to focus on first. It was nice of him to be so excited about teaching her to run, but giving her all those instructions at the same time was actually counterproductive. Reminding herself to keep a straight face, she let her husband's explanations wash over her, and moved her attention to the leaves on the trees stretching overhead. They were like an endless carpet in the hallway of some elegant mansion. Green. Yellow. Red. Evidently the trees all changed color at different times. It felt luxurious to be holding all three colors in her field of vision at once.

"Look how pretty it is," she said.

He looked up. "You're right," he said. "Aren't you glad we came?"

"Yeah. Thanks for getting me out here."

"Studies have proved that performance suffers when you don't take breaks."

Tomoko copied her husband, who was swinging his arms rhythmically, and looked at the pale, skinny, sticklike arms that peeked out of her running clothes. She needed to exercise more, it was true. She'd been putting in such long hours working that her fitness had suffered. Particularly her leg muscles. Now that she was out running, she couldn't ignore it. It was like having to drag along bloodless pieces of doweling.

"The leg muscles are one of the most prone to losing mass, of course. You should be walking daily, whether you go out for a stroll or even just for shopping." He sounded like a teacher lecturing a student.

Yes, Tomoko thought; that was definitely true. But what could her husband really know? Running into the cold wind, she thought back to the exhilaration of being a student and putting snow against her eyelids to keep herself awake while she studied for exams. Squinting into the clear autumn sunlight, she gazed at the figure of her husband running just ahead of her. How could he possibly know what it was like, when he didn't have a single muscle on him?

She saw a couple approaching, dressed in understated matching duffle coats and walking their dog. "Hey, look. Those two are actually old enough to be grandparents. So adorable," she said, in a low, affectionate voice.

Her husband slowed his pace. "Very elegant," he said happily.

Just like we want to be when we're older, right? Tomoko thought, but she didn't say it aloud, because she was sure her husband was thinking just the same thing.

Six months since they'd gotten married, she was only more certain that the path to happiness was laid out ahead of them. From where did she get this satisfying feeling that they had avoided the common pitfalls of choosing a partner? Theirs was a marriage that hadn't necessarily been welcomed by their loved ones, but now she felt that the wild birds were twittering to congratulate them on having made the right choice.

As she passed the old couple on the path, Tomoko tried to imprint their image into her mind. She and her husband would no doubt become like them. In the weekday park, everything shone brightly and was peaceful. The sunlight spilling through the trees. The fountains. Grass. And her straw husband. She sighed with happiness at her blessed life.

They spent the next fifteen minutes doing a lap around the spacious park, slow enough to avoid putting any strain on their hearts. Within the park's extensive grounds, everyone was enjoying themselves. A couple on a date, peering into a flower bed. Families relaxing on the grass. A student rehearsing lines on a bench, a cameraman shooting a scene as he scattered a pile of fallen leaves around a girl . . .

They were just past the park's dog run. Her husband pointed to a patch of grass and said, "Let's get to there and then take a breather."

Tomoko was already fast-walking more than running. "Okay," she said, summoning the remains of her willpower.

"I'll grab us something to drink. Go do some stretching."

Tomoko watched him sprint off toward some vending machines, and made for the grassy area, dead leaves crunching underfoot. A deserted, slightly balding patch of ground—that was the spot. When she sat down and arched her back as far as she could, her gaze met a totally cloudless sky. She closed her eyes against the brightness, and became aware of the sensation of her blood coursing through her. Her body had been tense from pressure at work, but it felt looser now thanks to the run.

By the time her breathing had settled, her husband came into sight from between the trees. He seemed to have gone a long way to find a vending machine. Unaware that he was being watched, he was walking slowly toward the patch of grass, clutching a plastic bottle.

From that distance, his jerky movements stood out a little, but Tomoko didn't mind. Her husband was made of straw—yes, *that* straw, stalks of dried rice or wheat, plant matter used as fodder for farm animals, or for their bedding—tied into bundles and rolled into a human shape.

Tomoko had married him of her own free will. Some of her friends had advised her to reconsider, but most people didn't even seem to notice that he was straw. What Tomoko had liked about him was that, as straw, he was kinder and more positive than anyone she knew. Of course, at the start, there'd been days when she'd barely managed to swallow food, sick with worry that they were too different, that she'd rushed into things. But now she no longer faltered in her conviction that her instinct hadn't led her astray.

The soccer jersey that her husband was wearing was more vibrant than anything else in the park. It was a beautiful yellow, representing the sun, which was the team's emblem. Meanwhile, her husband was more akin to a brush painting of a dead branch, and Tomoko couldn't help but laugh out loud at the contrast.

She saw her husband put the bottle down on the ground and leap up to catch hold of a pine bough. He did a pull-up, raising himself easily, and then resumed walking as though nothing had happened, picking up something from the ground and shoving it in his pocket as he did. *An acorn*, Tomoko thought. *Or some insect.*

Her husband noticed her watching him and waved. Tomoko waved back enthusiastically. *Over here!* No doubt he was smiling from ear to ear. Her husband didn't have eyes, or a nose, or a mouth, but sunlight cast minute shadows that rippled across his face, putting the observer in mind of different expressions. After sending a round of applause to a youth who was practicing juggling nearby, with a lightness of bearing that made it seem that he was about to be airborne, he started running toward the patch of grass where Tomoko was waiting.

On the drive back from the park, her husband said he wanted a latte.

"You want a warm one? Right now?" Tomoko had been looking forward to getting home and showering, but she said, "Sure, let's get one to go."

Her husband's beautiful fingers, rolled and tied as finely as any artisanal object, made contact with the car's turn indicator lever. As they turned left at the intersection where they would normally make a right, Tomoko let the car seat take the weight of her sweat-damp back.

"Are you getting hungry?"

"Not yet," Tomoko said. The strange voice her husband emitted from the gaps between his stalks of straw could be difficult to make out unless you listened closely. In the beginning, this had given Tomoko pause too, but now she understood him without too much difficulty. Her husband found a spot free in the metered parking lot, and cut the engine. At that exact moment, it dawned on Tomoko that a work problem on which she'd reached an impasse could be solved another way, and she reached for her phone to make a note of the solution before she forgot. She heard the driver-side door open, and unbuckled her seat belt to get out and follow her husband.

Just then, the car rang out with a sudden sharp clunk, as if a hard object had hit something. Still on her phone, Tomoko paid it no mind, but then her husband said, "What was that, that sound?" and she quickly brought her focus back to him.

"I don't know," she said. "Did something hit the car?"

"Nope. It was your seat-belt buckle." Her husband had opened the door on his side, and was paused awkwardly halfway through the process of getting out of the car. He looked down at the phone in Tomoko's hand. "Why do you have to be so rough with it?"

"I'm sorry," Tomoko said quickly. She had no awareness of having unbuckled her seat belt roughly, but then again, only last week she had opened the passenger-side door and accidentally bumped it against a guard rail. Her husband's car was a brand-new BMW that he'd bought less than a month ago.

Tomoko opened her car door. "That was the seat belt? That sound?"

"That's right. It hit the door just there," her husband said, leaning over into the passenger seat to inspect the spot. "See, look—here! Can you see the scratch?"

Tomoko couldn't, but she apologized again anyway. *There's no way the seat belt could have reached all the way up there*, she thought. Her husband was pointing out an area near the top of the window frame, insisting that it was damaged. *That line's probably just part of the car's design.* But she decided to wait until he noticed it himself. Once he had calmed down a little, she could casually say, *Why don't you check what it looks like on the driver's side?*

Her husband was still facing intently toward the window frame. "Come have a look," he said eventually. "See? It's dented."

It was as he said. There was a distinct two-inch-long groove along the top edge of the window frame. Tomoko traced it with her finger. "You're right," she said. "It does look like there's a little dent."

Tomoko slipped her phone into a coat pocket. "I'm sorry," she said, dropping her head slightly. "I wasn't paying attention."

Her husband was sitting very still, gripping the car's steering wheel. Tomoko couldn't read an expression in the dense layers of fine straw that made up his face, but she sensed he was grappling with silent rage.

Fearfully, Tomoko asked, "Did you want to go get your latte?"

"You let me down," her husband said with a sigh, and dropped his head to his chest.

Tomoko wasn't sure how to respond. Her husband raised his head again. After a while, he repeated himself. "You let me down." He sighed and once more dropped his head, leaning his body toward the steering wheel. "You let me down."

"I'm sorry. Really." Tomoko thought he might keep doing this movement endlessly unless she did something. "I didn't think a seat belt would reach that far."

She wasn't rewarded with a response. The uncomfortable silence, punctuated by the rustling sound of bundled straw repeatedly hitting the wheel, went on for several minutes.

Finally, as though snapping himself out of it, her husband announced that he was going to get his latte, and opened his door. Tomoko started to get up, but then thought that might make her seem uncontrite, and decided to stay in the car. Her husband, apparently, had had no intention of waiting for her. He crossed the road swiftly without even glancing back.

Once she was alone, Tomoko let out a deep breath. She gazed unseeingly at the number plate of the car parked in front of them, then got out her phone and quickly tapped in the rest of her note. She noticed a single stalk of straw that had fallen at the foot of the driver's seat, and was picking it up when her husband came back with his drink and started the car without a word. They made a U-turn and went back the way they'd come.

"I'm truly sorry. I promise to try harder in the future," she said, picking her words carefully. She wondered whether she ought to say more, but she thought it might be disrespectful to say things she didn't mean.

As soon as she looked out the window, though, she changed her mind, and put her hand on top of her husband's where it lay on his knee. Since getting married, she'd learned the hard way that it only made things worse when they didn't talk to each other. Her husband didn't react to her gesture, but Tomoko kept her hand there for a while.

Deep inside her husband's hand, almost imperceptibly, she felt something squirm.

Tomoko stared at his hand. *What was that?* To hide her alarm, she pointed to the latte sitting in the cup holder. "Can I have some?"

"Help yourself," her husband said, like an unfriendly receptionist. Sipping the warm latte, Tomoko thought about what had just happened. There'd definitely been something lurking within that straw. She felt something start to itch uncomfortably inside her brain. Maybe what she thought she'd noticed was just a vibration from the car.

In their living room, her husband said, "Let me down," and sat heavily on the sofa. Wondering whether it meant anything that he had dropped the "you," Tomoko sat as well, straight on the carpet.

Her husband was still slumped over, his upper body bent forward and his face in his hands as though he was struggling against despair. "Why do you have to be so careless?" he said. "I don't get it. It's not even a month old."

"It was an accident. It was the same last week. I didn't mean to. I just wasn't aware I had to be that careful when I unbuckle my seat belt."

Her husband seemed to be making an effort to understand. Still holding his face in his hands, he nodded repeatedly. But then, in a strained voice, he cried, "I don't understand," and started rocking his body back and forth, as though he believed it would make things more bearable. Subtly at first, and then harder and harder. As Tomoko looked on helplessly, he made a movement as if he were tearing off parts of his head, and got up and strode off toward the front door. Tomoko followed, and found him silently sweeping the floor of the entrance hall, which had just been swept two days ago.

"What are you doing?" she said.

"I don't know."

"Please. Stop." Tomoko took the broom from his hand, and led him by the arm back to the sofa. "I promise. I promise I'll be careful from now on."

"Sure." His voice was hollow. He started rocking again, and Tomoko watched until she started to feel like a boat drifting out to sea, too far to get back to shore.

"I don't do it on purpose," she said as patiently as she could. "Please. Just believe me about that."

"Maybe," he said quietly.

Once again, something moved swiftly inside his straw. There was no doubt this time. A fine tremor was running through her husband's body, traversing it from end to end. Tomoko almost cried out in horror, but her husband didn't seem to be aware of anything.

"Are you accusing me of being destructive deliberately?" She felt a duty to act as though she hadn't noticed what was happening.

"No, I'm not saying that."

It was as she'd feared. Around the area where a mouth would be, her husband's straw was quaking. Something was pushing on it from inside. Tomoko's eyes were glued to his face.

"I'm not saying that, but it's obvious that you think it's no big deal if the car gets damaged."

Every time he spoke, she felt she was about to catch sight of something from between the straw. Her husband's insides were teeming. What was in there?

"You already promised just last week that you'd be more careful."

"What I promised was about the door," Tomoko said, forcing the words out, desperate to keep the conversation going. "You know I've been really careful opening the door since then. But I just never thought I had to make sure not to let the seat belt bounce up and hit the door."

"Do you really need me to spell out every last thing?"

Just as he said "every last thing," something fell out of his mouth. Whatever it was, it seemed to have been swallowed by the deep pile of the carpet or, at any rate, was nowhere to be seen.

"I'll pay attention, I promise. I'll do better from now on."

"Can you give me a more specific strategy?" he asked accusingly, noticing Tomoko's less-than-heartfelt tone.

"A strategy? For being more careful?" Tomoko couldn't look away from her husband's face. Something had started welling up from between the straw—tiny musical instruments. An assortment of different musical instruments, barely large enough to pick up with the tips of her fingers, was flowing out of her husband. Trumpets. Trombones. Snare drums. Clarinets. Harpsichords. "A strategy for taking my seat belt off more gently?" she said quietly, distracted by the instruments.

"I mean, you don't actually feel it's a serious problem. When you open the door carefully, you only do it to avoid me getting angry about it."

Her husband was starting to sound enraged. Was that somehow related to the instruments falling out of his body? Tomoko said, "I feel like I've been doing it thinking I should treat the car well, but does it not seem that way to you?"

"I don't believe for a moment you think that." The flow of instruments sped up even more. They were piling up at his feet into a mound that almost hid his slippers. At the same time, her husband's body was shrinking.

"Why do you get to decide what I think?" On reflex, Tomoko thrust her hands out under his face, trying to stem the cascade of instruments, which showed no sign of stopping. "I think you want to call me a bad person. Then why don't you just say so? Why do you have to be so passive-aggressive about it?" Her hands filled up almost immediately, and hundreds of drums and flutes spilled over the edges of her fingers. "I'm impressed you could even marry someone you felt this way about!"

Her husband kept talking, causing an outpouring of hundreds of pairs of cymbals. "If you really—*crash*—felt bad about doing it—*crash crash crash*—you wouldn't even think about making excuses."

How? How could he not know he was spewing instruments?

The flow of instruments let up. Tomoko looked up quickly, and saw that the form of her husband where he sat on the sofa was utterly transformed. Bereft of his insides, he was now reduced to a pitiful amount of unstuffed straw. The string that had tied him together was loose in places, and he looked as though he might fall apart at any moment. Which was him? Tomoko wondered. The musical instruments that had fallen out of him, or the husk of straw that remained—which was her husband?

"Please, can we just stop fighting now?" she cried.

At this, her husband seemed to pause, and finally closed his mouth instead of saying whatever he had been about to say. In a cold, distant voice, he said, "You're right. Fighting's only a waste of time."

Tomoko looked into the black void that was now visible from between his straw. *He's out of instruments.* There were small piles of them on the carpet that added up to almost exactly the size of him—alto horns, euphoniums, marimbas. She gingerly tried to reach for her husband's hand. But her husband, apparently no longer able to support the weight of his soccer jersey, collapsed before their hands could touch, like a plant blown down by the wind. Tomoko grasped his limp hand where it lay. "It's okay. Don't worry. It's all my fault. I won't ride in your car anymore."

"Sounds good," he said weakly.

Tomoko realized that his scent, which had been as familiar and cherished as towels dried in the sun, had changed into the smell of animal feed. She stood up, and looked down at her empty husband as he lay still, with his back to her.

Inside her head, another Tomoko said, *Why did I get married to a thing like this? Why was I so happy to be married to a bunch of straw?* Her husband was utterly unmoving. Maybe he was already dead. *If I hit this body with something*, she wondered, *would it feel like there was nothing inside?* As she looked down at him, the picture of a fire burning brightly burst vividly into her mind. The image of something going up in violent flames on the stark white sofa, in the morning sunlight filling this room in this house. Tomoko didn't yet know what happened when you set fire to straw. How would it burn? Her heart beat faster just imagining it. Just a little flame would probably ignite it all in the blink of an eye . . .

Tomoko came to her senses. Unable to bear to see him like this any longer, she started to put the fallen instruments back inside the straw. She couldn't tell whether they were broken, but as she gathered them gently in both hands and poured them into the gaps, his body expanded like a sponge sucking up water. Tomoko repeated the movement over and over. From carpet to straw. From carpet to straw.

Just once during the process, Tomoko stopped and picked up a fallen stalk, and carefully touched it to the flame of an incense lighter. The flame reared up like a live thing. Tomoko sighed at its beauty, and thought about how she'd like to set a whole bundle alight like this sometime. She finished pouring the last of the instruments back into the gaps in her husband.

Eventually, her husband got up from the sofa. Seeming to have recovered his strength, he looked up at Tomoko and, casting subtle shadows on his face through its delicate ridges, gently said, "I'm the one who should be apologizing. It's just a car. I'm sorry I got so upset over it. Shall we go for another run?"

With her hand clasped in her husband's, Tomoko forgot that she had just been imagining a hunk of straw getting swallowed in flames. She accepted the invitation cheerfully. "Good idea. Let's go."

As they ran through the park, which was slightly more crowded than it had been earlier, Tomoko shifted her gaze up to the turning leaves, and murmured, "It's beautiful." The sunlight spilling through the trees. The fountains. Grass. Flower beds. She could hear a constant stream of instruments falling and breaking underfoot. Miniature French horns and timpani. As her husband taught her to run, Tomoko breathed in the cold air. The afternoon was lovely. The leaves overhead were as beautiful as burning fire.

© Rana Shimada

YUKIKO MOTOYA was born in Ishikawa Prefecture in Japan in 1979. After moving to Tokyo to study drama, she started the Motoya Yukiko Theater Company, whose plays she wrote and directed. Her first story, "Eriko to zettai," appeared in the literary magazine *Gunzo* in 2002. Motoya won the Noma Prize for New Writers for *Warm Poison* in 2011; the Kenzaburo Oe Prize for *Picnic in the Storm* in 2013; the Mishima Yukio Prize for *How She Learned to Love Herself* in 2014; and Japan's most prestigious literary prize, the Akutagawa Prize, for "An Exotic Marriage" in 2016. Her books have been published or are forthcoming in French, Norwegian, Spanish, Korean, and Chinese, and her stories have been published in English in *Granta*, *Words Without Borders*, *Tender*, and *Catapult*.

ASA YONEDA was born in Osaka and studied language, literature, and translation at the University of Oxford and SOAS University of London. She now lives in Bristol, U.K. In addition to Yukiko Motoya, she has translated works by Banana Yoshimoto, Aoko Matsuda, and Natsuko Kuroda.